THE WITCH AND THE HAIRBRUSH

N. S. HOWARD

MELANGE BOOKS, LLC

ONE

Mijestic took long strides down the wood plank sidewalk, her high heels making splinters fly with each step. People moved out of her way, recognizing her as a witch. She could not legally put spells on others without a permit, but there wasn't any point in risking that technicality. Her black outfit, one of the many Witches' Guild requirements, identified her as a witch.

In truth, Mijestic didn't exactly follow the traditional garb for witches. Today, her outfit comprised stilettos, a mini-skirt with fishnet stockings, lace gloves and a bustier that barely contained her bouncing bosom. Her hat had a point to it, but it was small with a discrete brim. The black clothes were in contrast to her pale skin, soft blue eyes, and long, fiery red hair. Her youth was also apparent in her maturity, or rather the lack of it. She looked and acted, like a twenty-year old. A twenty-year old brat with a temper.

She strutted past the window of a brick building, which proclaimed in gold paint and antique lettering, 'The Government Offices for Permits and Licences'. Just past the window, a wood door stood with an 'Open' sign hung in the middle. Mijestic flung open the door and marched past the twin rows of counters standing in the middle of the room. Each counter had paper forms arranged neatly with quill pens secured by strings. She made a straight line for the end of the room where wickets with metal bars separated clerks from the rest of the room.

Paper forms flew in the air as she stormed through. A clerk, dressed in a white shirt and a pinstriped vest, watched her approach and crossed his arms. He was as tall as she was, older looking, but with a calm demeanour. She found his stern face and black hair with grey streaks imposing.

She stopped at his wicket and pointed at a small red blemish on the tip of her nose.

"Do you know what this is?" She didn't wait for a reply. "It's an ugly pimple that's a result of a curse placed on me."

He raised his eyebrows. "That is most unfortunate."

"Unfortunate!" She began to shout. "I want to know who did this."

He casually pointed with a finger to a small sign next to wicket that read 'This office does not tolerate loud, rude or insulting behaviour'.

She looked up the ceiling, sighed, and lowered her voice. She didn't want to risk having her name placed before the town Justiciar again for unruly behaviour. "Who filled out the permit to put this curse on me?"

"I regret to inform you we do not divulge that information."

Mijestic pounded a fist on the counter. "This is so unfair."

"I'm sure you're quite right, madam, but we only process the permits and accept payments for such."

She spun on her heel and charged out of the office, causing another flurry of paper forms to float in the air.

Mijestic wasn't sure of her next destination. There were several shops in the town of Elfwind where a person, with the right permit, could have a curse or spell placed. The fees varied, and also the guarantees, for such services. Privacy was assured, although a bribe, or a threat, could loosen a tongue. Unfortunately, she wasn't sure which shop it would be, if one was used at all. Even if she took the trouble to purchase a permit, she could cast a spell herself, and there were a good number of magic practitioners who could perform simple spells.

The blemish she woke up with could well disappear on its own, depending on the spell. More likely, she would have to go through the Book of Spells, Potions and Curses to find the correct antidote. What bothered her was that anyone would not think of her in the highest regard, and would take the time to put a spell on her. No doubt someone jealous of her good looks, intelligence, good nature and social standing.

She began to walk aimlessly down the sidewalk, trying to think of anyone who didn't think of her as perfect.

"Mijestic."

She turned to the feminine, if slightly low, voice. Accalia was a few inches shorter than Mijestic, but of the same weight. She kept her dark brown hair shoulder length, which helped frame an oval face with full lips. She wore a collar, in this case a red one with spikes, which identified her as part of the Werewolves' Guild. The matching wrist cuffs, however, identified another activity she indulged in.

"Hello, Accalia. How are you feeling now?"

"A lot better, thank you. Last Saturday was the worst day ever."

Mijestic gave her best friend a hug, forgetting her own problem. It was an unfortunate set of circumstances that led to Accalia being put in a cage for a day. Besides having an argument with her boyfriend, the time of the month led her to being an emotional wreck. There are few things worse than a werewolf, a full moon and a bad PMS day. Ryder, the alpha male in her pack, got tired of her whining and growling and locked her up in a cage for the night at his home.

"Was Richard mad at you?"

"He was pretty upset when he had to pick me up on Sunday. First, he made me walk home naked with a leash on. It's a good thing we could return home by walking by the Great Forest. I think no one noticed us. When we got home, he gave me a helluva spanking with a wood paddle."

Accalia was one of the exceptions of a creature committing herself to a human. It was difficult for her, for she had to obey the alpha male and the alpha female in her pack, and that sometimes conflicted with the wishes of her partner, Richard. The relationship worked because Richard was willing to work with her pack when she could go out and accepted she was under their control during that time. The pack also understood Accalia was Richard's submissive and tried not to put her in a position where she might have to disobey him.

The town's council decided all mythical creatures had to belong to a guild, and each guild had to accept the town council's rulings. Thus there was little worry of a werewolf attacking a vampire or an elf turning a ghoul into a frog with the Justiciar handing out strong disciplinary measures.

"Ouch." Richard was big and strong. A paddle in his hands would be a painful instrument. She understood Accalia was submissive, willing to wear restraints and receive discipline from him. "So, what are you up to?"

"I just came from dropping some chicken noodle soup to Theron."

"I heard he came down with the flu."

"Yeah, I guess that's the danger when you suck on other people's blood. You can catch whatever they have."

Mijestic didn't come across Theron too often, as he was always indoors during the day. But the vampire had a great sense of humour and could be the life, or at least the undead, and soul of a party. Being tall, dark and handsome, he attracted a few ladies who were willing to let him nibble at their necks. He had to be careful he didn't bite the same victim too often, or she could end being a night prowler herself. Theron was also the president of the local Vampires' Guild, a small Guild because vampires were territorial. All members wore a traditional cape and agreed not create any new vampires.

"I hope he'll be better soon."

"I'm sure he will. Vampires have a strong immune system and recover fast from most things. Where are you going, Mijestic?"

Mijestic explained the pimple on her nose and how the permit office wouldn't help her. "I just want to ask whoever did this why they did it. I mean if I actually did something wrong, it would be nice to know what it is. Now I've got to find the remedy. Stupid, anonymous curses."

"Oh, a pimple isn't so bad. Remember when Victor was made into a donkey for an afternoon last year? And how about Venus, when her clothes disintegrated right on Market Street? Of course, she didn't seem to mind very much with that body of hers."

"There were rumours she had that spell put on by herself to generate some publicity for that new book she wrote."

"Oh yeah, that book supposedly exposes what really happened on those Roman religious festivals."

"Come on, let's check out the courtyard square and check if there's anyone we know that will be punished."

Mijestic agreed, for a half penny it could be fun entertainment. The courtyard was in front of Town Hall and protected by a stone wall waist high with a decorative iron railing on top. An iron gate at the front was open during the daytime, and visitors paid to watch those being punished for their crimes. There were four pillories and four posts for those who were to receive discipline, and in the corner a hanging pole. There hadn't been a hanging for years, but the town council liked to leave it in full view as a deterrent against the more serious crimes. Murder, rape and throwing eggs at the mayor's home were considered criminal enough to warrant the death penalty.

They inspected the list of those to receive punishment and noted they were in time for the paddling of Lady Jacquelyn. Mijestic and Accalia each dropped a half penny coin in the collection pot and walked to where pillories were placed in a square. In front of each pillory and post was a board with a parchment stating the name, crime, and punishment of the guilty party. They walked among the small crowd of people looking at those found guilty of crimes, keeping on the brick pathway. It was considered a serious breach of protocol to cross the lawn where the discipline was being carried out. Vendors in push-carts sold lemonade, hot food and pastries, giving the courtyard a festival appearance.

Two of the stockades were already in use, but none of the poles. Mijestic read the inscription on the first document out loud, "Nicholas, fresh vegetable merchant, accused and found guilty of selling spoiled fruit. Justiciar ruled that he be placed in a pillory for three hours."

Accalia pointed out that Nicholas, a middle-aged, shirtless gentleman of thinning hair, had already been subject to some additional punishment. He looked uncomfortable as he leaned forward with his head and hands inside the wood block. "There's a bin of tomatoes here, and it looks like some have already been thrown at him."

Red juice dripped from his face and around him on the pillory.

Mijestic picked up a couple of tomatoes. The first one she hurled missed the target completely, but her second hit him square on the forehead.

Accalia clapped her hands and picked up a pair of tomatoes as well. Both her throws missed, but she grabbed an armful of tomatoes and tossed them at Nicholas. One hit him in the face and another sailed over the stockade and hit him on the back.

Mijestic and Accalia laughed and moved on to the next pillory.

Accalia read the description in front, but there was little doubt what the brunette woman's crime was. Lilith was charged and convicted of adultery, which meant being placed in a pillory. She was also naked, and while initially a white sheet was placed over her back, it either slipped or had been pulled off by an adventurous visitor. A red letter "A" had been painted on her shoulder.

Mijestic asked Accalia, "Do you know her?"

"No, but I've seen her before. Pretty girl."

"Yes, she is. It's remarkable how it's always the woman charged with adultery."

"I think it's an excuse to have them naked." Mijestic guessed how the Justiciar perceived things. If he was married, and she wasn't, then she must have seduced him, for a married man was always true to his wife. If she was married, and he was not, she was obviously being unfaithful. Mijestic noticed there were several people having a good look at the unfortunate woman.

It reminded her of the time she was accused of casting a spell without a permit. Being a witch, she didn't believe she needed a permit to cast a spell. The Justiciar disagreed and fined her the cost of a permit plus disciplinary action in the courtyard. If she'd been a male witch, she likely would have been whipped. But being a woman, her wrists were tied above her head to a pole for an hour. She was also stripped naked, and could only stare back at the amused faces of the crowd. Actually, she wasn't embarrassed by her exposure and even aroused at the attention she was receiving. She didn't, however, appreciate the cat call from her two older sisters, or the spanking she received later from her mother.

"You haven't been convicted of a crime for a while now, Accalia." Accalia, especially a few years ago, had difficulty keeping out of the Justiciar's notice.

"Yeah, the last time was a few months ago when I got caught doing some mischief as a wolf. I got the usual punishment for a woman. Stripped naked, and they attached a chain from my collar to a post."

They walked to the next stockade and Mijestic commented, "I think a lot of women end up naked for public display on some silly crime. Not many men though."

"Yeah, but the men get whipped. I'd rather be naked. They gave me the option of paying a fine instead of standing around naked, but I needed the money more than my dignity. I'm a werewolf, so I'm used to being naked."

"You're a good looking woman and a beautiful wolf." Mijestic gave her smile, knowing how self-conscious Accalia was about her human body. Werewolves had a tendency to keep a muscular and heavy boned anatomy after changing into their human shape. For female were-wolves that often meant a body without the normal curves and smaller breasts.

The crowd call out and they turned to watch a blonde woman escorted by two guards, each dressed in the blue uniforms of the police service. One of them carried a wood paddle. The tall, slimly built woman wore a simple white shirt that barely reached to her thighs. Her wrists were tied in front of her by a rope. She walked bare-foot with her head held high, twisting away from one guard's attempt to guide her by the arm. The three marched past the pillories and to a pole where she showed little reaction to her wrists being secured above her.

Mijestic commented, "We've seen her before."

"Yeah. Lady Jacquelyn's is the wife of the gold merchant, Lord Montagu."

"I thought the rich would be immune to the Justiciar."

"They usually are, if they want to be. Lady Jacquelyn has been here before with silly offences. I think it's something Lord Montagu and she enjoy doing."

One guard read out the offence for which she was charged. "Lord Montagu has accused his wife, Lady Jacquelyn, of using a sharp tongue with him and showing the lack of respect a wife should show her husband. Lady Jacquelyn pleaded guilty to the charge and thus has been sentenced to ten strikes on her posterior."

One guard folded up the bottom of her shirt, taking care not to touch her skin, and knotted the fabric so it stayed above her waist. The other guard poised with the paddle near her bare bottom.

Mijestic watched as each strike made by one guard was counted by the other guard. It seemed to Mijestic the first guard was not putting full force into the blows, although her cheeks still turned pink.

The two guards left her tied to the post with her shirt still tied up to her waist. Lady Jacquelyn twisted around to look back at the crowd, not looking displeased with her audience.

Accalia spoke, "I told you. She enjoys being paddled in public. The rich must get bored easily."

Mijestic bought two pastries from a vendor pushing a cart to share with Accalia. They walked past the poles and Lady Jacquelyn being returned to the town hall.

"That was fun, but I better be getting back home. Richard won't be happy if I'm late getting home again. I told him I would only give Theron some soup."

"All right. Want to go for a drink tonight?"

"Sure, why don't you come around my place after dinner? Richard likes it when I'm with someone when I leave the house."

Mijestic sat at the dinner table with her mother and sisters. She ate slowly, careful to chew her food and observe the rules of dining her mother enforced.

Her mother looked, and dressed, like someone in her mid-twenties. There were several advantages to being a witch, including being able to use a youth spell, and Lucinda made sure her daughters understood them. She also stressed the traditional aspects of being a witch and was troubled by Mijestic's attitude. True, Mijestic wore only black, but it was one of several rules she twisted around so she could do what she wanted.

Lucinda's other daughters were better behaved, although each had minor issues. Gwendolyn had long black hair like her mother and almost as tall. She favoured short skirts with slits, long sleeved lace blouses that were see-through, and didn't like to wear undergarments. Gwendolyn also enjoyed wearing the only colour witches were allowed, the red striped stockings. Her mother tried in vain to express that was meant to be socks only, but Gwendolyn wore them as stockings with a garter belt.

Selena, a petite blonde, in some respects was the more traditional witch, and took an interest in the making of special potions and spells. She often helped her mother in making dinner and cleaning of the house. Her dress and skirts were almost always full length and her top of heavier cloth. She was also a lesbian, and in the Witches' Guild that could be an advantage as there were far more females than males. A witch could take a partner outside of the Guild, subject to the approval of the Guild executive, but it was difficult to find outsiders who wanted to stay with a witch.

Many people in the town of Elfwind preferred to stay with their own species. Over half of the town comprised normal people with no special characteristics or powers. The rest, werewolves, vampires, witches, warlocks, ghouls, changeling, satyrs, elves and other creatures had their own guilds and rules, with a tendency to keep with their own.

Lucinda took a drink of her wine and cleared her throat to get Gwendolyn's attention. "This Saturday we'll be going to the Guild meeting. As the treasurer of the Guild, I need to set a good example to the other witches. That means we'll respect the spirit of the dress code for witches. Your skirts will be long and your blouses will not be transparent. Bras and panties are to be worn. They're not an option. Do you understand that, Gwendolyn?"

Gwendolyn nodded. "Yes, Mother."

Lucinda next directed her attention to Mijestic. "You may have bare legs or black stockings, but not fishnet. Is that clear?"

"Yes, Mother. Boring clothing only."

Lucinda sighed, "Really Mijestic, fashion does not have to be a statement every moment. I believe I'm very tolerant of you and Gwendolyn expressing yourself."

She looked at Selena. "Dear, I don't want you to trying to make new friends this time. This is the last meeting before Walpurgis Night and we need to focus on planning for the event."

"Yes, Mother. I understand the spring ritual is very important."

Lucinda smiled, believing she had made the message clear. "Just to be certain, if I'm disappointed in any behaviour, I'll use the hairbrush on your bare bottom. None of you are too old to be put over my lap."

Mijestic cringed. Of all the daughters, she'd received the hairbrush the most.

TWO

Mijestic took her older broom on her evening with Accalia. It wasn't as fast or manoeuvrable as her new one, but she didn't want to risk damaging it during a night of drinking. She rode the broom side-saddle for the sake of maintaining an ounce of modesty.

The broom, under Mijestic's control, flew quickly down the streets. She took a couple of shortcuts over a vacant lot and a general store closed for the evening, although it was illegal to fly a broom anywhere but roadways. It couldn't be said that Mijestic liked to play it safe.

She parked her broom at the front door where Richard and Accalia lived, a yellow brick home whose backyard faced the edge of town where the Great Forest started. She knocked on the door.

Richard, tall, broad shouldered, and with a hint of stubble on his face, opened the door. He kept his sandy coloured hair short and neat. Mijestic noticed before that being neat extended to his clothes, home and workshop. Accalia received several disciplinary measures for leaving what Richard considered a mess until she learned what he expected.

"Come in, Mijestic." He stepped aside. "Before you go out, there are a few rules."

Mijestic smiled at Accalia sitting in the living room. She wore a dark green sleeveless top, black jeans and a black leather collar with a leash attached. Accalia gave Mijestic a grin.

Richard spoke. "I don't want this to be an all-nighter. You are to bring her home by midnight. She must wear a leash and you, and only you, are to hold the other end. Keep her out of trouble for a change. Agreed?"

"Sure." Mijestic gave him a smile.

He didn't look impressed. "If there're incidents, both of you will suffer the consequences."

Mijestic took the end of the leash. "Sure. Later, Dick."

She heard him take a deep breath and she stifled a giggle.

Accalia hopped on the broom behind Mijestic. "Don't go too fast. I don't have the same balance on this thing as you do." She put her hands on Mijestic's waist.

"The faster you go, the easier it is to keep your balance."

Accalia let out a shriek as the broom accelerated, snaking down the road. A few horses and another pulling a carriage were startled as they whizzed by them. A horse rider shook his fist at them as they flew past and caused the horse to rear up. Mijestic laughed as the broom climbed higher. The wood handle vibrated as the broom pulled more power to lift the two women. They flew over a home and followed the road to one of the market streets, arriving at a tavern called The Elephant and Rook. Mijestic carried her broom inside the noisy bar with one hand and Accalia's leash in the other.

It told a lot about the town's inhabitants, and their way of life, that a witch holding the leash of a werewolf didn't bring undue attention. The two women brought enough attention that they didn't have to pay for any of the many drinks they consumed. Mijestic, in particular, was not opposed to allowing her skirt to ride up her leg as she sat on a barstool. She found when the top of her stocking was exposed, the offers and drinks would come faster, and she made sure most of her leg was visible. A tall man tried to start a conversation with Mijestic, but she ignored his efforts, although she was intrigued by his aristocratic attitude and looks.

"Allow me to introduce myself. My name is Lorhon."

"Mijestic." She gave him one of her practiced flirty smiles.

"Let's share one drink together." His voice rumbled as he leaned on the table by her side.

"Sorry. Not this time." She continued to smile as she surveyed him. He was handsome with a strong jaw and steel-blue eyes. Dark hair and a shadow on his face gave him a rugged, bad boy appearance.

He left her alone, but she continued to watch him as he walked up to the bar to order a drink. As he stood there, a pretty blonde came up to him and started a conversation.

He looks good, and I doubt he'll be going home alone tonight.

The evening turned into night, and after sharing a serving of bat wings, Accalia and Mijestic staggered out of the tavern.

Accalia laughed as she climbed on the broom. "That was fun, but it's near midnight, so I better get home."

The broom made wild turns down the street, occasionally going over a home. Mijestic laughed as they almost collided with a couple walking down the street and she yelled out an apology. Eventually she brought the broom to rest at the back of Accalia's home.

"Hey, I want to go for a run. Would you like to go for a ride?" Accalia began to undress.

"What kind of ride are you talking about? Do I need to get undressed too?"

Accalia giggled. "Maybe later. Just hang on to the leash and ride your broom." She changed into a wolf, and with her pink tongue sliding over pointed teeth, looked back at Mijestic. She let out a howl, began to sprint.

Mijestic was always amazed how fast a werewolf could change states, reforming when they wanted. At one time the werewolves were limited to changing into a wolf once a month during a full moon, but intense lobbying by the Werewolf Guild managed to get the town council to change some natural laws. It helped that the mayor was a wizard of considerable power. There was now a minimum of five full moons per seven nights, the remaining phases of the moon spread over the other three days. An acute observer will note this adds up to eight days a week, however the town council also created an extra day one minute long that occurs between Saturday midnight and Sunday morning. Nonday, as it was termed, was a convenient day to put unpleasant events in. Major storms, for example, were by law ordered to occur only on Nonday. An additional advantage was those who drank too much on Saturday night had an extra day to recover.

Mijestic held on to the leash with both hands. The wolf raced along the clearing between the homes and the forest. She couldn't sit on the broom side saddle any longer and had to hitch up her skirt to lock her legs around the broom's shaft.

The broom zigzagged after the wolf. Suddenly the wolf changed directions by jumping over a fence and running through the backyards of the homes. Accalia leaped over fences and hedges, spraying mud and flowers as she sprinted. Residents appeared in the backyards, some shaking their fists at the wolf and the witch.

Mijestic almost flew off the broom when the wolf leaped. Her top was also having difficulties and gave up trying to contain her breasts. Her bustier became bust. She didn't care, leaning back on her broom with her breasts exposed, laughing with delight.

The ride came to a stop as the wolf, panting, made its way home.

Accalia changed back into human form and gave Mijestic a hug and a kiss on the cheek. "Now that was fun."

Mijestic agreed. "We must do that again soon."

"Come on in for a drink." She placed a finger to her lips. "Be quiet. Richard might be asleep."

Mijestic followed her inside. She tried to fix her top but gave up, deciding if Accalia was naked, she could be topless. She unbuttoned her bustier and tossed it on the couch, plopping next to it. She took the clear liquid drink from Accalia and coughed as the drink burned her throat.

"Wow, what is this?"

"Something Richard buys from a guy who runs his own still." She sat next to Mijestic. "You're a great friend. Thanks for the evening. I needed to let my hair down."

Mijestic put her arm around her. "To friends." She took another swallow, this time not finding the drink as harsh.

Accalia responded. "To friends." She put her drink on the floor and spread out on the couch, resting her head on Mijestic's lap. "I think I'm very drunk."

"So am I." She stroked Accalia's hair.

"You have nice boobs. Big, but not too big. Nice, dark nipples. I wish I had boobs like that."

Mijestic laughed. "Your boobs are just fine." She cupped one of Accalia's breasts.

Accalia stretched out her hands above her head. "I liked it when you held my leash tonight. I felt protected and under your control. It was like part of a fantasy I have." She sat up. "I'll get you a blanket. You can sleep on the couch."

Mijestic nodded, not wanting to fly the broom home. She was curious what Accalia's fantasy was about, but decided she would ask another time.

Meanwhile across town Constable Moe Thursday, badge number 417, inwardly grumbled as he listened to Lord Montagu speak about his latest complaint concerning Lady Jacquelyn.

"She totally ignored my request to keep the home dust free. I even provided her with a maid but, as you can see, to no avail." He gestured to unseen dust around the room.

Thursday looked at the large room with dark wood floors, polished to a bright shine. The cream coloured walls held several large oil paintings, all of damsels in distress, and with heavy drapes covering the bay windows. The furniture was a sturdy looking with floral patterns on the chairs. It could be said it had a French influence, if France ever existed in the same realm as Elfwind. However, what attracted Thursday's attention were the two ladies on the floor.

The maid was wearing an abbreviated black-and-white uniform as she lay on her stomach on the floor. The hem of the short skirt was resting above her hips, showing off her garter and black stockings. Her black laced panties had been pulled down to expose red cheeks. Her hands were tied behind her back with her ankles crossed and tied together with a rope to her wrists. The final item of note was a red ball gag. Next to her, Lady Jacquelyn was identically tied, except she was naked and on her side.

"Yes, sir."

"I want Lady Jacquelyn charged as such and disciplined by the Justiciar."

"Yes, Lord Montagu. I can write up a charge, unless Lady Jacquelyn has a statement."

"Emmmumm."

"I shall assume no objection to the charge then."

"Urmmmum."

Lord Monteau nodded. "Excellent. The failure to provide a clean environment should be considered a serious offence. I recommend that she be stripped nude and be given a sound paddling in the Town Hall courtyard, perhaps with some nipple clamps added."

"Eruruuummm."

"Just the facts, ma'am." He pointed at the maid. "And her, sir?"

"We'll, that is, I will take matters into my own hands concerning the... hired help."

The maid whimpered.

"Very good, sir. I shall be on my way."

Thursday headed to the East end of town, not pleased Lord Monteau was using the police and the Justiciar to satisfy his, and Lady Jacquelyn's, perversions, although there was little he could do about that, as Lord Monteau was in good social standings with the mayor and the Justiciar. Thursday looked forward to his next call where a disturbance of a werewolf and a witch were seen to be the cause. This at least looked like an actual law was broken and he could use his keen detective skills to catch the perpetrators.

After he arrived in the neighbourhood, he noted the lights still on in three of the homes, and those residents were all too willing to give their opinions of the events. Thursday wrote that a werewolf pulled a witch by a leash as she rode a broom over the open field and the backyards. The wolf was hard to identify, as one wolf looked a lot like another. He examined the churned up gardens while listening to "You must do something," while not given any information on who the witch or the wolf were. However, he received a break when he interviewed an elderly gentleman who stood transfixed as he stared at the open sky in his backyard.

"What did you see? Could you identify any of the alleged criminals?"

The old man sighed. "She was leaning back on her broom. Bare breasted. Her nipples...oh such a sight."

"Yes, sir. Did you recognize the perpetrator?"

"It was majestic." He sighed again.

"Mijestic? Can you name the wolf?"

"Just majestic." The old man continued to stare at the sky as his hand reached toward the horizon.

Thursday flipped his notebook closed, pleased with his discovery of the name of the witch. She had been the source of much conversation among the constabulary. Mijestic was suspected frequently of using magic and spells without a permit, and her reckless broom flying was a hazard to all. On top of that, her arrogance and lack of respect to the police, who were only doing their low-paying job, made her to the top of the "I want to send to the Justiciar," list. Thursday suspected the werewolf was Accalia, her accomplice on many of her criminal activities. He hoped they could force a confession out of Mijestic and have her name her friend.

THREE

Mijestic fluttered her eyes open to the sound in the room. Through blurred vision, she watched Accalia, wearing one of Richard's shirts, pick up a bottle and glasses from last night. Mijestic slid her feet off the couch, letting the blanket fall to the floor where her skirt and bustier rested. A vague memory came forward of Accalia helping her take off her skirt and kissing her goodnight several times. She inspected her stockings and was pleased to discover they didn't have a run in them.

"Good morning."

Accalia gave her a smile. "More like good mid-morning. Richard has been up for hours and went to town to get some groceries. He'll be back soon."

Mijestic nodded and began to dress. She found her shoes across the room and put them on. "I guess I better get home."

"You can't. Richard is upset and wants to talk to us. That likely will end up in a spanking for both of us."

"Not me. He's not touching my bottom."

Accalia frowned. "He usually gets his way."

A noise occurred at the backdoor and next in the kitchen. Richard soon appeared in the living room, wearing blue jeans and a white t-shirt. He sat in an armchair and faced the two women.

"I'm not happy with what happened last night. Accalia has caused some damage to the backyards and gardens along the block. I suspect an official complaint has been made to the police."

"Sorry." Accalia held her head down.

"Sorry." Mijestic returned his gaze from the couch.

He pointed at Accalia. "Strip and come over here."

Accalia took off her shirt and walked over to him. She didn't hesitate lowering herself on his lap.

Mijestic watched as Richard's big hand come down on her ass, striking each cheek numerous times. Accalia rested her hands on the floor, occasionally kicking her feet, as her cheeks turned red. She cried out, but didn't ask him to stop or offer any resistance. Mijestic's lips parted as she stared. She had seen her sisters spanked by her mother before, but the sight of Accalia being spanked by Richard was entirely different. Her sisters being spanked was funny to her, depending sometimes if she was also in line for a spanking. But this spanking appeared erotic. She watched as Richard shifted Accalia on his lap so her head nearly reached the floor, placing her ass even higher. His hand came down again, reddening even her thighs. Mijestic took a deep breath as she wet her lips.

After a lengthy spanking, Richard helped Accalia stand. "Now stand in front of the wall on your toes with your hands behind your back."

Mijestic saw tears run down her cheeks as Accalia quickly complied.

"Now for you, Mijestic. Take off your skirt and come here."

"You're not my master." Mijestic's voice quivered. "You can't order me around and I didn't really do anything wrong."

He stared at her. "I left you in charge of Accalia. You were to have her home by midnight and keep her out of trouble. You failed completely in that regard. Do you disagree with that?"

His voice had a deep sounding command to it that made her pay heed. She answered quietly, "No."

"Then if you fail to keep your promise, don't think you should be disciplined? No consequence at all?"

"That's not fair." Her voice was soft. She looked to floor. "You're making like it was my fault."

"Perhaps it is. Did you consider that?"

"I don't know." Her voice stuttered as she looked back up at him.

"It's up to you. What's your word worth?"

"Damn it." Mijestic stood and slowly removed her skirt. *I would prefer it if he just grabbed me and threw me over his lap rather that getting me to submit to him. This is more humiliating.* She took small steps to where he waited. "I'll accept my punishment."

He took her arm to help her rest over his lap. She thought, although her black lace thong wasn't offering any protection or coverage to her ass, at least he wouldn't hit as hard as her mother did with the hairbrush.

She was wrong.

Mijestic realized several sensations. One was the impact of his hand that covered almost her whole cheek with each blow. The second was the jarring of her body that translated into her breasts easing out of the bustier. Once again, the bustier took leave, but that was the least of her concerns as the pain shot up her backside.

She kicked her feet, sending her shoes flying one at a time across the room. Desperate to slow the spanking, she reached a hand behind her to cover her backside. He grabbed her wrist, twisting it behind her back and pulling her against him.

That was when she another sensation occurred, namely his erection pressing against her hips.

She wasn't surprised of his arousal, but was startled to discover of her arousal as well. A warmth was pulsing in her groin and she was sure she was wet. She hoped it wasn't obvious to him.

He stopped. "I believe that's sufficient punishment for failing to live up to your promises."

"Thank Frodo." She noticed he still hadn't released her.

"But now you need to be disciplined for arguing with me."

"You can't do that." Mijestic whined and soon found out she was quite wrong on that point.

Mijestic cried out, "I'm sorry. I promise to be good. I'm sorry. I'll obey. I'm sorry. Please stop. I'm truly sorry." The second spanking hurt worse than the first.

He finally stopped, resting his hand on her ass. "Now go to the wall with your hands behind your back." He helped her stand.

"Yes, sir." Mijestic hurried to the wall and began to pull up her bustier.

"I said, hands behind your back. Leave your top alone and stand on your toes."

She immediately put her hands behind her back, not worrying about her fallen top. The spanking was humiliating, and her arousal was annoying. She heard Richard's footsteps leave the room and turned to look at Accalia. She was surprised at her grinning and trying to stifle a giggle. Suddenly Mijestic found a laugh trying to creep out and bit her lower lip. She looked away from Accalia, knowing she was ready to laugh out loud if she continued to stare at her.

Finally, after long minutes, Richard announced they were to come to the kitchen.

Mijestic and Accalia entered the kitchen with their hands behind their backs.

"Sit down and eat breakfast."

Mijestic sat, conscious of her exposed breasts and, much to her annoyance, erect nipples. She decided she hadn't been given permission to touch her top and didn't want to risk another spanking by pulling it up. Mijestic filled her plate with eggs, cakes, and sausages and began to eat. The wood chair initially felt cool to her burning cheeks, but now was making the pain worse. She tried shifting around to ease the pain.

Richard spoke to her. "The next time you'll be naked for your spanking. Understand?"

"Yes."

"Without argument or there'll be an additional lesson."

"Yes, sir. There won't be any argument." Mijestic lowered her head. He scared her and she realized she would obey him. She also suspected, judging by her history of learning her lesson, there would be a next time.

After breakfast, she helped Accalia clean up the table and wash dishes. She received permission from Richard to dress, she quickly fixed her top. The skirt was a different matter; the tight leather hurt her sensitive skin as she carefully pulled it up. The ride home on her broom was slow as she replayed the events of the morning, wondering about her feelings. *That spanking left me wanting something else as hard as this broom between my legs. I hope Mother doesn't learn what happened last night, or learn of my spanking this morning.*

Her mother was waiting for her when she returned home, holding a yellow piece of paper.

"A town enforcement officer dropped this off for you."

"Oh?" She tried to give an innocent look that came off as someone who had just dropped an expensive wine glass.

"Riding on a broom topless while with a wolf, causing a disturbance and destroying private property. Those are the charges. You are to appear in front of the Justiciar tomorrow morning to answer them." Lucinda crossed her arms. "What in Middle Earth's name were you up to last night?"

"I, well, that is, it seems..."

"Try the truth, young witch."

"I got drunk with Accalia. She changed into a wolf and began to run through some backyards and I followed her on the broom."

"Topless?"

"My top fell down by accident. Honest."

"This is right before our Guild meeting about Walpurgis Night. Don't you have any sense at all?"

"Sorry, Mother."

Lucinda took a deep breath. "To your room. I'll deal with you shortly."

Mijestic shuffled to her room and tried to figure out a healing spell for her bottom that wouldn't be detected by her mother. Most spells left an unmistakable odour of ozone and caused a slight change in temperature. Lucinda was adept at knowing if a spell was used close by. Mijestic was still tempted to try a small spell when her mother called for her.

She entered the living room, not surprised by the grinning faces of her sisters. Her mother stood, holding the famous hairbrush in her hand.

"Please, Mother, I'm very sorry for what happened."

"Good. In a minute you'll be even sorrier." She stood with her arms on her hips. "Off with everything below the waist."

Mijestic sighed. She knew there wasn't any point in arguing. She didn't hurry as she took off her shoes, skirt, garter belt, stockings and her thong. She walked over and bent over, resting her hands on her knees. She thought of the wide, oval hairbrush poised in her mother's hand, the dark brown wood had worn to a softer colour on the flat side. The black bristles were all straight, and Mijestic determined it had never been used to brush hair. The hairbrush was old, handed down from her grandmother, making it a rather painful family heirloom.

Lucinda began to wind up her swing, when she stopped. "What ever happened to your bottom?"

"Accalia's boyfriend, Richard, spanked me."

"It looks like he did a splendid job. His fingers left marks."

Mijestic's sisters laughed out loud.

"I'll be easy on you this time because of that."

Mijestic learned that didn't mean she was getting away completely, but eight strokes later she could return to her room and put on something that "wouldn't cause difficulty when sitting," as her mother told her. She picked a loose, pleated black skirt, and nothing else underneath. She spent the rest of the day carefully sitting and being quiet.

Mijestic wished she could use a spell to get rid of the ticket, but that wasn't possible. She was still worried about the pimple on her nose and decided it was as good a time as any to look for a cure.

Mijestic hauled the massive Book of Spells, Potions and Curses to the dining room table, dropping it with a thud. She'd heard some witches and warlocks had all the spells in the book memorized, but had trouble believing anyone could live long enough to do so. She flipped open the book, skimming over the pages containing the ISBN number, first printing date and other technical details. Then there were a dozen pages of acknowledgements to other practitioners of magic, and the author's humble thanks to her editors, before she got to the table of contents. It was divided into two sections, one for spells and making potions, and a second section for counteracting everything in the first section.

Mijestic groaned as she scanned the listing for cures for skin disorders that covered two pages. It's just a pimple. What's the simplest counter spell here? She frowned. *What if I use the wrong counter spell? Will that make things worse?*

She came to a conclusion on what to do. "Mother! I need help with a spell."

Lucinda and Selena came into the dining room from the kitchen where they were working on various potions.

"What's the problem, dear?" Lucinda peered at the book on the table.

"I'm trying to figure out a spell to remove the pimple on my nose."

Selena giggled. "Don't worry, Mijestic. The pimple will just turn into a wart. It'll look very natural on a witch."

Mijestic whined. "Make Selena go away. She's not helping."

Lucinda ignored her daughters, resting a long fingernail on a counter spell. "Try this one. It should work and won't cause any side effects. Really, Mijestic, you should spend more time studying spells. What would you do if I wasn't around?"

"Oh, I would help her, Mother." Selena chimed in. "You can trust me."

"Right." Mijestic decided she better learn spells, if for no reason other than to protect herself from Selena. Selena was the oldest of the three daughters and sometimes decided she was in charge when their mother was away. Selena would use spells to force her two sisters to do what she wanted and wasn't above handing out discipline herself. After Mijestic was left alone, she tried the spell her mother had suggested, stumbling over the words of the ancient, beautiful language.

Є пляма я потребую позбутися

Чи викликаний відрізком часу або не.

Зробіть це imperfection поїдьте Таким чином

я буду красивий ще раз весь день.

Mijestic hurried over to the mirror at the front entrance, checked her reflection and gave a shout of joy. She jumped up and down. "It's gone! It's gone."

Accalia came over to the house in the evening after dinner. Mijestic invited her in for a tea, but she declined.

"I'm so sorry you got into trouble because of me. I'll confess to the Justiciar it was me that caused the problem. They'll go easier on you that way."

Mijestic shook her head. "Don't you dare. They'll just punish you and still discipline me that way. It's okay, I'm sure I'll just have to stand naked in the courtyard for a few hours. Maybe some guy will like what he sees and ask me out later."

Accalia laughed. "Not the best way to meet a guy." She gave Mijestic a hug. "I better get back home. Richard let me come over to apologize, but otherwise I'm grounded. He will make me stay in my kennel tonight and I'm guessing another paddling is in order."

"Try not to let him figure out you enjoy those spankings, or he will make them really hard."

"Good point." Accalia waved goodbye.

Mijestic was worried about the sentence she would receive from the Justiciar. The police suspected her of several other minor offences but never had sufficient proof to charge her. She was sure they would do what they could to have the prosecution push for strong punishment.

FOUR

Mijestic's mother travelled with her to the Town Hall the next morning. She also helped pick out her daughter's clothing, choosing a long skirt, a simple blouse with a high collar and low-heeled shoes.

The Town Hall, a stone rectangular building three stories high, contained the offices for town administration, including the justice department on the second floor.

They waited in line for a wicket to be available and stepped forward to present the summons. The official barely looked up at them, stamping the summons and told them to go to room 212. That room was a seating area for those charged, with a few of the simple two dozen chairs being used. Mijestic recognized one of the accused, Lady Jacquelyn, as she sat next Lord Montagu. Both were well dressed, although Lady Jacquelyn wore a white peasant blouse that left her bare from the shoulders up. This accentuated the black leather collar she wore, complete with a padlock. Her wrists were tied together at the front with a thin rope. She still had a dignified look and stared back at anyone who looked at her too long.

Mijestic sat with Lucinda, exchanging a few whispered comments. Occasionally a female clerk would open a door at the far end, call out a name, and the reluctant participant would follow her to the courtroom beyond.

Mijestic's name was called, and she made her way across the room with her mother, leaving Lady Jacquelyn and Lord Montagu behind.

The Justiciar, a heavy set, middle-aged man with thinning hair, sat behind a bench on a raised platform. He was dressed in a black gown with a white shirt underneath. Lucinda and Mijestic waited at the far end of the room until her name was called again, and they approached him with their heads bowed. A guard stated the charges and the prosecutor, a blonde woman wearing a black robe over a red dress, gave the official version the crime commented.

"Your honour, this is a most serious crime. Property wilfully destroyed. Drunken behaviour. Disturbing the peace late at night while good, law-abiding citizens were trying to sleep. Public nudity. Failure to stay within the roadways while flying a broom. Your honour, we need to send a strong message that this total disregard for our laws will not be tolerated."

The Justiciar nodded his head. "You have made a very strong argument for the prosecution." He peered at Mijestic through his round glasses, making his blue eyes appear large. "Do you have any justification for breaking these laws?"

Mijestic swallowed. "I didn't mean to cause any problems. I may have had too much to drink and made a couple of mistakes."

The prosecutor jumped in. "A couple of mistakes? Obviously, your honour, she still thinks destroying gardens as a mere inconvenience for the poor, suffering victims. However, before we ask for punishment for the wide range of these hideous crimes, I'll give Mijestic an opportunity to redeem herself." She pointed a finger at her. "Who was the wolf that accompanied you on this crime spree? We strongly suspect it was Accalia, but we need you to confirm it. Give us that name and we'll reduce the charges."

Mijestic shook her head. "I won't give you a name."

The prosecutor frowned. "Very well, you've brought this on yourself. We ask the Justiciar to consider these measures to help deter future crimes. First, for the public nudity offense, we ask that Mijestic be stripped naked and secured to a pole in the courtyard. Because she apparently likes to expose her breasts, we recommend the addition of nipple clamps."

The Justiciar leaned forward. "Oh, yes, we do like that sort of punishment."

"Also, for causing a disturbance and flying outside the roadway, I recommend the defendant be paddled twenty times."

"A paddling. Noted." He licked his lips.

"For the destruction of private property, we recommend a whipping of not less than ten strokes on the back."

"Good, good. That would be a strong deterrent."

The prosecutor smiled. "Finally, because Mijestic refuses to divulge the name of the wolf she was with, the prosecution asks that a crotch rope be used during her time in the courtyard."

The Justiciar smiled. "That's a unique, and possibly the best, suggestion you have made for some time."

"Thank you, your honour." She blushed.

He turned his attention to Mijestic. "Do you have anything to say before I pass a sentence?"

Mijestic was speechless. She was expecting be stripped naked, and perhaps even given a paddling, but the punishment was far beyond what she expected.

Lucinda spoke up. "Since when is a woman whipped? Does she look like a man to you?"

The Justiciar nodded. "A valid point."

"I would also like to remind the Justiciar that the Salem Treaty prohibits harsh punishment of witches, such as burning at the stake or excessive paddling. Twenty strokes are too much."

The Justiciar frowned. "What do you suggest for punishment?"

"I'll accept her being stripped naked and paddled four times."

The prosecutor gave a rebuttal. "Ten strokes, and I insist on the crotch rope, unless she gives up the name of the wolf. Also the nipple clamps, unless she accepts an additional paddling. I think the nipple clamps are a nice touch and should be used more often."

The Justiciar nodded. "I like the nipple clamps, too." He looked at Lucinda and Mijestic. "Do we have an agreement?"

Lucinda looked at Mijestic as her daughter nodded her head, giving out a feeble, "Yes."

"Then the sentence is passed. The defendant shall report in four days' time at sunrise to the basement of Town Hall." Frowning at Mijestic, he added, "You shall be placed in a cell until it is time to be taken to the courtyard. You will be taken naked with the nipple clamps to the courtyard where you will be secured. An officer will administer ten strokes with a paddle. You will then have a crotch rope attached. You will be left that way for one hour. Do you have any questions?"

Mijestic shook her head. "No, your honour."

"Good. I'm looking forward to seeing your punishment. Strictly as an impartial observer of justice, of course."

The prosecutor agreed, "Oh yes, it'll be quite interesting to see." She stared at Mijestic and grinned.

Lucinda walked with Mijestic home.

"You're the daughter that has caused me the most grief and worry. Actually, I thought you would be in front of the Justiciar far more often than you have been, so maybe this makes up for the times you escaped punishment."

"I suppose so, Mother. I'm sorry I've embarrassed you. Thanks for speaking up for me and taking away some punishment."

"You're welcome. A mother must protect her children as best she can. But you didn't embarrass me and I was proud of you when you refused to give up Accalia's name to reduce your own punishment." She put her arm around Mijestic's shoulder and gave her a hug. "You may have your faults but you always had a good heart."

FIVE

The lodge for the Witches' Guild was a large wood structure and tonight it was filled with witches for the last meeting before Walpurgis Night.

Mijestic sat with her sisters near the front of the hall at a circular table with eight chairs. Food and wine were at each table and Mijestic snacked as she chatted with others. Her mother, the treasurer for the Guild, gave a report on the finances and concluded with a wish the Walpurgis Night would be another grand success.

Mijestic wasn't comfortable in her conservative clothes, but decided against disobeying her mother's wishes. She forced herself to pay attention to President Helga's speech about special arrangements being made for Walpurgis Night.

"We shall not run out of the nectar of the earth this year as I've personally obtained a sufficient supply of the liquor, I mean nectar. I shall remind everyone that white robes are available for sale for a reasonable price. Please contact Secretary Roseanna about purchasing them."

Walpurgis Night was one of the few occasions when witches weren't required to wear black and must wear the white robes. As the night progressed, the nectar of the earth, drugs and spells began to have an effect, and soon the robes were shed. There were rules for the orgy that followed, which basically meant one couldn't refuse the advances of another witch. The problem for Mijestic was there were more female witches than male.

The meeting ended and Mijestic slowly stood. Her cheeks were still sore, and she was not looking forward to the paddling she would receive at the courtyard in a day's time.

Mijestic's unavailability because of the meeting had consequences for Richard. Accalia was determined to attend the latest courtyard festivities and watch the latest punishment of Lady Jacquelyn. Richard was suddenly, and reluctantly, drawn in to escort Accalia. He preferred to work at home rather than observe what happened to those who broke the law.

"I mean, she acts so snobbish and so deserves to be punished in public, even if the charges are a bit made up." Accalia continued to chat away about how the courtyard punishments were becoming more popular, making it a good source of revenue for the Justiciar and the town. "They're making the punishments more unique and I know some guards for their style of using the paddle or whip."

Richard agreed with her. At one time the courtyard was free to attend. Then came the quarter penny charge and later the half penny charge. Children were now only allowed in during the morning sessions and to be accompanied by an adult.

There was a line up at the entrance to the courtyard. A sign advertised there were four events for the afternoon entertainment. Besides Lady Jacquelyn's punishment, a female witch was to be stripped and paddled for using a spell without a permit, a male werewolf was to be whipped for mischief, and a barmaid was to be stripped and left exposed for stealing.

Accalia took Richard by the hand to the first post. Richard read the notice that the barmaid, Alalyn, was convicted of pocketing money that belonged to the Blue Garter Tavern. It was further stated Alalyn would keep her job and work weekday evenings. He looked up the barmaid, a middle-weight brunette with long, curly hair. Her wrists were secured together above her head, while her ankles were spread apart by a pole. Richard thought Alalyn looked excited at the attention she was receiving and watched her smile at a man in the audience.

Accalia commented. "I think this conviction is a scam. This is the fourth barmaid this past week to be convicted of stealing, and none of them punished other than being stripped. I think they use the naked females to attract business for the bar."

"I think you're right. She doesn't seem to think it's a punishment, anyway." Richard walked to the next station where a man was facing a pole without a shirt and pants, standing in only his underwear. He had a hairy back and legs, which was typical of the male werewolves. Accalia looked at the signage posted and shrugged.

"It doesn't say what mischief he was up to. He might have been just marking his territory by peeing on someone's property."

"Do you know him?"

"Draven. I met him a couple of times at social functions as a wolf. He's not bad looking from the back. Good muscle tone."

"Most werewolves have strong muscles. And a desire to run around naked."

Accalia turned to smile at him. "It's just natural."

An announcer proclaimed that Draven's punishment was about to begin. "Let's give a round of applause for Cassandra, one of our new up-and-coming torturers."

Accalia looked at Richard. "They're using more women now to punish those convicted of crimes. I guess it has something to do with gender equality hiring."

They listened to the clapping as Cassandra, a tall, slender, bronzed-haired woman, entered the inner courtyard carrying a black, coiled whip. Richard noticed she was also a catwoman, identifying the feline face and claws at the end of her fingers. He couldn't see her ears, but knew they would be short and pointed. Their collar, which had a small bell attached also identified catpeople.

Cassandra waved at the crowd and grinned with small pointed teeth showing. She flicked the whip open, letting the length unravel on the grass. She snapped the whip a couple of times and she turned her attention to the man secured to the pole.

Cassandra pulled her arm back and let the whip fly. Her aim was true and a red stripe appeared on Draven's back. She didn't hesitate to strike him a second time, and he sagged slightly after the blow.

Accalia whispered, "I hope she doesn't hurt him too much."

Richard nodded and looked on as several more marks were made on his back. Then Cassandra shifted her attention to his legs with two more strikes. She turned to the crowd and gave a smile, receiving applause. Cassandra gave a small bow of her head and returned her attention on Draven. She dragged her arm back and then let loose with several short swings, leaving the back of his underwear in shreds and exposing his backside.

Cassandra took a deeper bow to the strong applause and walked up to Draven, whispering something in his ear and patted his ass.

"I wonder what she said to him." Richard asked.

"She looks like a hussy. Werewolves and catpeople have a hate, love relationship. Some can't stand the other, but others are fascinated by the other species. Since she's a catwoman, and he's a male, I suspect she made a suggestive comment to him."

"I know you don't really like catpeople."

"I hate catwomen. Some catmen are okay, as long as they understand I'll never obey them and if I catch them under a full moon, they better run."

Richard walked with Accalia to a pillory that held a naked woman. The witch, a medium built woman with chestnut hair, was waiting for her paddling. Once again, the announcer shouted out the next event and a guard came out with a black leather paddle to the inner court. He was a slender man, but used both hands to swing the paddle. The effect was a loud slap of the leather smacking the witch's skin. He took turns hitting from one side of the witch to the other. After the fifth hit the victim cried out, her ass now a bright red. The guard was undeterred by her pleas and finished the ten strikes, leaving her cheeks a mottled, bruised red and a dark blue. Richard wondered if that was like the punishment Mijestic would receive and recalled she would also get additional attention.

An announcement broke his thoughts. "Ladies, gentlemen and creatures. Our featured performance today is about to start. Lady Jacquelyn is to be disciplined by one of our senior guardsmen, a man appointed by the Justiciar himself to carry out this duty. Please, put your hands together for Tony the Terror."

Cheers erupted as the crowd looked on to where the convicts were led from the town hall. A dark skinned man with grey hair led Lady Jacquelyn by a rope around her neck to the courtyard. She was naked save for a silver collar and a set of silver nipple clamps with a chain between them. Her hands had been secured behind her back and she was led to the inner courtyard to a position between two poles.

Tony the Terror marched like a military officer, and Lady Jacquelyn had to quicken her steps to keep up. She still kept her head up high, not looking embarrassed or defeated, although her eyes were wide open as if she wasn't sure what to expect. When they reached the inner court- yard, Tony the Terror placed Lady Jacquelyn between two posts. He released the rope that secured her wrists together at her back and tied each wrist to a posts, stretching and lifting her arms. She gave a small gasp as he secured her last wrist, and she had to stand on her toes to help relieve the pressure.

Tony the Terror strode around her, holding up the cluster of birch in his gloved hand. He gestured at the crowd, but didn't change his stern face.

As the crowd cheered, Lady Jacquelyn peered around. She was breathing hard, looking unsettled.

Tony the Terror stood behind Lady Jacquelyn, holding the birch. He took his time, waiting as the crowd became quiet. Then he struck, the birch striking her ass. Many torturers used a first blow or two to test their swing. But his first blow was full force. Lady Jacquelyn let out a cry. The second and third blows left her ass red.

Richard watched as she balled her hands into fists. *She's hurting.*

Tony the Terror made several more strikes on her ass, and on the back of her legs. Lady Jacquelyn jerked against her restraints and howled as the birch struck her inner thigh. Tony the Terror smiled at her torment and marched around in front of her. He waited as Lady Jacquelyn showed signs of recovering and focused on his hand holding the birch.

"Please, stop." She whimpered.

Tony the Terror merely lifted his arm waist high, holding it there as the audience held their breath. He pivoted, sweeping the birch across her stomach.

Lady Jacquelyn gasped just as Tony the Terror reversed his swing, brushing her breasts. He took a step to the side and used the birch once on the front of each thigh. Lady Jacquelyn gave out a small cry as he tossed the birch to the ground and raised his hands in the air to great cheering from the crowd. He waited for a moment as he faced his fans and took a deep bow.

Finally, he untied her wrists from the ropes. With tears streaming down her face, he led her back to the town hall as applause and cheers followed their footsteps.

Richard watched them leave. "I suspect she learned her lesson."

"Perhaps, although Mijestic and I figure she enjoys her punishment. This was more severe than what she had before."

He took her arm and led her to the exit. "She may not be the only one who likes some discipline."

Accalia blushed as they walked. "Sometimes I do." She pointed at a sign. "Oh my gosh. I wonder if Mijestic knows about that."

Richard looked at the large sign pinned to the exit gate.

SPECIAL EVENT
SEE THE WICKED WITCH MIJESTIC PUNISHED
SEE THE PADDLING
SEE THE NIPPLE CLAMPS
SEE THE CROTCH ROPE
HER DISCIPLINE HOSTED BY THE TALENTED ENYO
PLUS—SEE OTHER EXCITING PUNISHMENTS
NOTE: THIS A PREMIUM EVENT- ONE PENNY FOR ADMISSION

"Does Mijestic know about this?"

Accalia shook her head. "I don't think so. If she did, she sure wouldn't be thrilled about it."

———

Lady Jacquelyn smiled sweetly as a servant escorted two more ladies to the gazebo, located in the middle of a flowered garden. She had planned her tea party several days ago, right after her appointment at the courtyard. She looked forward to the questions about her ordeal and, if prompted, would reveal part of her still red cheeks and breasts. Lady Jacquelyn had practiced how to look embarrassed and humiliated by the discipline initiated by her oppressive husband. Now that all four guests were seated, and the servants had retreated to the edge of the garden, Lady Jacquelyn spoke quietly and looked down at the table.

"I almost called off our little afternoon tea. I was so humiliated by ... yesterday's experience." She looked up at the others seated around the white laced table. "However, I decided I would not let the actions by Montagu stop me from my commitment to hosting our tea." She waited for their response and their comments on her public birching. Lady Jacquelyn knew they had been present at the courtyard to witness her discipline, having paid a gnome to inform her of those in attendance. She had earlier sent her acquaintances a note telling them of her sentence, and the exact time and date, and trusting they wouldn't think less of her because her punishment.

Lady Katherine spoke, "Oh my dear, Jacquelyn, we do understand. How you endure Montagu's controlling nature and remain his wife is a wonder to us all."

"Thank you for your kind words, but I vowed to love, honour and obey. My public discipline is something I must accept."

Lady Adonia reached over and patted Lady Jacquelyn's white gloved hand. "I witnessed the horrible beating you received from that brute, Tony the Terror. I forced myself to watch the entire beating, wondering when it would end."

"It did look painful, but have you heard what they're going to do to that witch Mijestic?" Lady Erica paused for a moment as the table turned their attention to her. "The poor thing will be paddled and have crotch rope placed on her. She's always in trouble with the law, but this seems so extreme."

Lady Katherine covered her ample mouth in surprise. "When is this going to take place?"

"Tomorrow afternoon. They're charging a full penny to watch it, calling it a premium event."

Lady Lydia shook her head. "This is excessive punishment, no doubt. I'm planning to observe this barbaric act, and if it's as bad as it sounds, I will write a strongly worded letter to the mayor."

Lady Adonia agreed with her. "These punishments do seem quite harsh. I just wonder how far they'll go."

"Perhaps it's what she deserves." The others turned their attention to Lady Katherine. "I mean we don't know what she did, so perhaps the punishment is justified. Certainly we need some deterrent for crime, and if the crotch rope will teach her a lesson, then I'm for it."

Lady Jacquelyn listened to the conversation go from about her to the Mijestic's upcoming punishment. *No discussion on my nudity, the nipple clamps or the birching. My humiliation completely ignored. What's wrong with these women? Do they think I invited them for tea to talk about that witch getting disciplined?*

Lady Erica put down her teacup. "Well, I have to say some of these women do deserve a good paddling. Perhaps if their husband, or boyfriend, would put them over their knee, they would learn proper behaviour instead of relying on the Justiciar to do it. I think the Justiciar is tired of seeing same people going in front of him and decided to increase their punishment. It could be the nipple clamps and crotch rope will become more common for repeat offenders." She looked at Lady Jacquelyn. "Oh dear. I do hope your husband knows that if he sends you in front of the Justiciar again, you may end up with a crotch rope."

Lady Jacquelyn sniffed. "If Montagu decides I need further discipline, I shall accept my fate. If they decide to use a crotch rope on me, there's nothing I can do about it."

Lady Jacquelyn fumed as she paced around the conservatory room floor, a highly polished hardwood that made walking in the red stilettos an adventure. The colour of the shoes matched the leather cuffs on her wrists and ankles, and the posture collar locked around her neck. Her long black dress had mesh in the front that constricted her breasts and was open below the waist at her back that showed off her red striped bottom.

A maid stood by the door, wearing a black-and-white uniform that wasn't long enough to cover her frilly black panties. The other part of the uniform comprised fishnet stockings, high heels and a black leather collar. She listened and watched Lady Jacquelyn carefully, knowing there a possibility she could be on the receiving end of her anger.

"Can you believe the nerve of the Justiciar giving that witch top billing over me? I get birched while spread eagle and naked, only to find everyone is talking about her getting a crotch rope. My tea group barely mentioned my humiliating punishment. It was so embarrassing being ignored like that." She turned to glare at the maid. "I'm so angry right now."

The maid, Evelyn, swallowed, wishing she was polishing silverware. The other servants had found useful tasks to do, and suddenly Evelyn found herself the attendant for Lady Jacquelyn. That involved massaging cream on her inflected areas, but also following Lord Montagu's orders regarding her what she was to wear. He gave written instructions to Evelyn, and Lady Jacquelyn would not dispute his requests, although she was peeved that a servant was telling her what to wear. Evelyn was in a difficult position. There were additional instructions Lord Montagu left that required Lady Jacquelyn being taken downstairs to the Purple Room, restrained and special devices added. Evelyn didn't mind setting up Lady Jacquelyn for Lord Montagu's pleasure later, but sometimes there were consequences for her. It was important to let the servants understand their rightful place, and Lady Jacquelyn enjoyed dishing out discipline as much as receiving.

Lady Jacquelyn was known for taking out her unhappiness on the servants, and right now, she was very unhappy. Evelyn hoped nothing would happen until she could announce to Lady Jacquelyn it was time to go downstairs.

"Do you have any suggestions, or perhaps I should take my frustrations out on you?"

Evelyn swallowed, the collar squeezing her neck. "Perhaps, Lady Jacquelyn, you could have someone place a spell on her."

"Hmm. That's a possibility. What type of spell?"

"You could hire a gnome to find out more about her and then decide on a spell. Perhaps hire a demon. They can do nasty spells."

Lady Jacquelyn nodded. Gnomes were the go to creatures to gather information. They were hard to detect, could sneak around and remembered almost everything came across. Demons would do any spell for the right price. "Good, that's what I'll do." She crossed her arms. "Now, take off those panties and bend over that armchair. I'm still upset."

Evelyn sighed. She had an hour before she was to take Lady Jacquelyn downstairs, and until then it could be most unpleasant.

SIX

Lucinda escorted Mijestic to the Town Hall, leaving her at the lower level where those convicted of crimes were held.

After signing an admission of guilt and absolving the Justiciar of any complications during her confinement, Mijestic followed the female guard to a cell. The guard, a slim medium height brunette with short, straight hair, stood by the open door. She wore a police uniform with pants instead of a skirt.

"Strip off your clothes. You'll remain naked until it's time to take you for your punishment. At that time we'll secure your wrists before taking you to the courtyard." She smirked at Mijestic. "You witches think you can get away with everything. I'm so looking forward to seeing your punishment."

Mijestic began to take off her clothes. "You're just human?"

"No special adaptations. I'm human and proud of it."

"Big deal. You're jealous. I'm a witch. Live with the fact I'm better than you and have a better life. Bitch."

The guard glared at her. "A better life? I'll remind you of that when I attach the nipple clamps and crotch rope." She took the clothes Mijestic handed to her and slammed the door.

"Guards are supposed to be impartial during the punishment." Mijestic returned her stare.

The guard laughed. "In what world is that?"

Mijestic paced around the small cell. It held a bed, a combination toilet-sink and a table. She saw the other prisoners waiting to be taken to the courtyard, two men and three women. The women, like herself, were naked and looked nervous. The men, without shirts, stood around and looked at the women.

The female guard returned at intervals, along with a male guard, taking away two of the women and one of the men. The guards appeared to be satisfied employees, looking proud as they took prisoners to the courtyard. Eventually they returned for Mijestic.

The female guard smiled. "Time for your appointment." She opened the cell door. "My name is Enyo, and I'll be your torturer today. Gregorios is a new guard and is here for training purposes."

Mijestic sighed and crossed her arms. "Whatever." She looked at Gregorios, who had a badge on his shirt with the word 'Trainee'.

"Cross your wrists behind you. The fun is about to start."

Mijestic wasn't sure about the guard's definition of fun, but it seemed to be the opposite of her own. After her wrists were tied with more rope than Mijestic thought was necessary, Enyo used a second rope to pull her elbows together. A rope to tie the elbows wasn't common, and she presumed it was at the guard's discretion.

Mijestic grunted as her shoulders were pulled back and her breasts pushed forward.

"There, that will help you keep your back straight and give good posture." Enyo admired the effect on Mijestic, nodding her approval. She held up a pair of black iron nipple clamps, attached by a chain. "These might hurt. Because they're heavy, I must tighten the clamp more than usual. I'm sure you understand why."

Mijestic became annoyed at the time it took attaching the nipple clamps. Enyo played with her nipples to make them erect before adding the clamps. It also involved Gregorios standing with his tongue hanging out. Mijestic frowned, knowing there was little point in offering any objections. After the nipple clamps were attached, she reflected her own pretty set was far lighter than the iron set that now encompassed her.

Enyo finally looped a rope around her neck, tied it and used the loose end of the rope to lead Mijestic out along a narrow hallway.

Mijestic muttered unpleasant thoughts about Enyo leading her out to the courtyard and wanted to use a spell to make Gregorios lose his eyesight as he panted behind her.

They stepped past the oak door into the courtyard. Mijestic blinked from the bright sunlight as she followed the guard. Suddenly, applause and cheering filled her ears. She took a moment to take in the large crowd that had paid to be in the courtyard and the realization she was the centre of attention.

An announcer called out, "Ladies, gentlemen and creatures. Our main event today is about to start. Let's give Mijestic a warm welcome."

The cheering increased.

Enyo turned to speak to her. "It's a big event. The nipple clamps are not uncommon, but it's the first time in years the crotch rope has been used. Together, they are causing a sensation among the visitors."

"Wonderful. What's wrong with people they want to watch me being punished like that?"

"I'm just happy you're punished. You've gotten away with too much. Always skirting the law and not getting caught. This crowd that came to watch you suffer a paddling is great. The crotch rope and clamps are just an added benefit."

Mijestic decided against saying anything more, not wanting to get the guard upset. She didn't want to further antagonize Enyo who would add the crotch rope later.

The crowd grinned and waved at Mijestic. It seemed there would be big profits for the vendors today, thanks to her public punishment. Mijestic saw Accalia, her mother and sisters. She also recognized the tall stranger, Lorhon, that she had seen at the Elephant and Rook, and he was securitizing her from behind the main crowd.

Enyo led her near a pole. She made a show of gesturing at Mijestic with one hand and then curtsied.

Mijestic rolled her eyes at the burst of applause, wishing everything could be done as quickly as possible.

The rope around her neck was tugged down to an iron ring secured to the ground and Mijestic had to bend over as it was tied. It was hard for Mijestic to observe, but she glimpsed Enyo holding a wooden paddle high in the air to the delight of the crowd. The guard enjoyed playing with the audience, making a few sweeping motions in the air with the paddle.

"Help me, people. Count out the strikes," Enyo shouted.

Mijestic felt the first solid smack as the crowd gleefully cried out "One." It hurt. The guard could really swing a paddle, and Mijestic blamed that on special police training courses.

By the fifth paddle, Mijestic guessed her ass was red. The nipple clamps were also causing some pain as they swung with each impact of the paddle. When the seventh strike was called out, she wanted to cry out to Enyo to stop, although that would be a waste of breath. Mijestic tried moving her ass to reduce the impact but Enyo, was patient, waiting for the right moment to deliver the final blows. Her cheeks had gone from sore, to painful, to being numb.

Applause and whistles broke out as the guard took a bow for the spanking.

The announcer came to life again, "And now, what we're all waiting for, the crotch rope punishment. Take it away, Enyo!"

Enyo removed the rope around Mijestic's neck, allowing her to stand up before turning her around and tying a rope from the ring in the ground to her wrists. She held up a coil of rope to Mijestic and the crowd.

"Spread your legs, Mijestic. Being a professional, I want to do this right."

Mijestic knew she had to comply, hoping without any reason that Enyo would be easy on her.

The rope was wrapped around her waist several times before coming up from behind and between her legs. It was looped through the rope around her waist and pulled snug.

Mijestic moaned as she watched Enyo take the rope and loop it high around the closest pole. She pulled on the rope, watching Mijestic as she did so.

Mijestic gasped as the rope tightened. She lifted herself on her toes, trying to reduce the pressure. Enyo made more gestures to her and receive applause, becoming more annoyed with the guard and her flamboyant style.

She looked at the crowd and was pleased to see her mother giving a look of encouragement. Her sisters, true to sibling behaviour, giggled at her predicament. Accalia gave her a smile and blew her a kiss.

Gradually Mijestic's ass began to come to life, throbbing with pain. It wasn't so bad as to make her forget the pressure of the nipple clamps and came a poor second to the crotch rope. So far, she had kept the pressure down by standing on her toes, but eventually she would tire and the rope would then make her life very uncomfortable.

She recognized a few other people, including Lady Jacquelyn, who looked jealous. She glared at Mijestic with her arms crossed. Lady Jacquelyn's had a good crowd to for her courtyard punishment yesterday, but was now upstaged by Mijestic's audience. Fame could be fleeting.

Mijestic gazed Lorhon, who was looking at a vendor selling hot goat meat on a stick. Curious, because she had nothing to look at but the rope tied to the pole in front of her, she studied the cart to figure out what he found so interesting. The cart didn't appear to be any different from the other carts and she failed to understand his fascination with it.

Suddenly an orange flame burst from a burner in the cart, followed by black smoke. The smell of burning goat meat, not the most delicate flavour to start with, began to drift over the crowd. The crowd's attention shifted to the vendor who frantically waved at the flames and smoke with his apron.

Mijestic grinned, finding it funny how everyone was running around the burning cart. It was then the crotch rope suddenly loosened. She slowly lowered her feet, as the tension on the rope disappeared. She looked back at the crowd, with Lorhon giving her a quick salute with his hand, before leaving the courtyard.

Only a witch or a warlock would know that kind of magic and seeing he's not wearing black, that means a warlock. That was clever to set the cart's stove on fire. It provided a diversion, and no one could smell the ozone from the spell. I've got to thank him for that.

The Witches' Guild didn't permit witches to associate with warlocks.

Warlocks had their own Guild, but their rules differed greatly from the witches'. For one, they only had to wear one item of black, be it a shirt, a skirt, or even just underwear. They could use spells in any way, as long as no one died, broke a bone, or lost an eye. The other difference according to the Witches' Guild was that they had no morals at all.

Right now Mijestic didn't care about that. She just wanted to kiss the handsome stranger for his help.

The time passed slowly for Mijestic. After the cart's fire was put out, things returned to normal. The crowd thinned out, although there were new visitors to stare at Mijestic's unfortunate position. Enyo finally returned to remove the crotch rope.

"Hey, I thought I had this tighter than this."

"Perhaps you have to go back to boy scouts to learn how to tie a knot."

"Girl guides. I went to girl guides." Enyo untied the rope.

"Sorry. Hard to tell. You look gender confused." Mijestic figured she could get away with a few barbs now that the punishment was over.

Enyo glared at her. "I'll remember that the next time you're back here." She took Mijestic back to the cell.

Mijestic learned that the removal of nipple clamps could be as painful as when they're put on. She also learned that if you insult a guard, there's an excellent chance some of your belongings may become lost. She left the town hall wearing only her top, which barely reached her hips.

Her mother scolded her for insulting the guard as they walked home. "You should've known better, Mijestic. They can be most unpleasant."

"I know that now. Did you see the tall man was that was in the crowd? Good looking, wearing a blue shirt?" Mijestic was curious if her mother would confirm he was a warlock. There was a chance he was an independent practitioner of magic.

Lucinda frowned. "He's a warlock. Stay away from him. He uses spells as if they were free and treats his women poorly. He's never done one nice thing in his life. He should be banned from Elfwind."

"But there isn't any other place other than Elfwind."

"Exactly."

SEVEN

The witches, all wearing white robes, met at the hall before going to the appointed field to celebrate Walpurgis Night. The president made a short speech, reminding everyone to act responsibly, as well as orgies could contain responsible behaviour, and to respect nature by cleaning up afterwards. She held up a piece of paper, showing the proper permit had been paid for and led the way to the forest where a path would take them to an open meadow.

The witches followed in clusters and occasionally in single file during the narrow parts of the pathway. A few carried torches which added to the festive mood for the witches. Mijestic was looking forward to the event, securitizing the other witches as she searched for the best male partners to end up with. She suspected the other female witches were likely doing the same thing. When the dancing started it required planning to end up with a good partner.

After a good walk, made more difficult because everyone was barefoot, they came to the chosen spot. Helga lifted her arms in joy as she made her way to centre of the field where she had previously stacked firewood. The fire was important as part of the ceremony, with the additional benefit that the smoke helped keep mosquitoes away.

Suddenly Helga froze. Black robed warlocks made their way to her wood pile.

The president charged forward, ordering the warlocks away. "Oberon, what are you doing here? Get your warlocks away from here now."

The president of the Warlock Guild, a tall black man, laughed at her.

Mijestic and the other witches looked on the ensuing argument. Gradually the warlocks and the witches stood in a line near each other. She wondered who would prevail.

"Nice to see you again, and fortunately, under better circumstances."

Mijestic looked up at Lorhon and blushed. "Yes, thank you for your help."

"Lorhon."

"I remember your name. We met in a bar before."

"Yes. Mijestic, such a lovely name. Pity your group will have to find another field."

"Why us? We've a permit and got here first."

He grinned. "Doesn't matter. We don't even have a permit. But we're the bad ones, and we don't have to be reasonable. We'll stay here and celebrate Walpurgis Night. If you're still here...Well, let's just say we don't mind mixed company."

Mijestic smiled at him. "So you don't want to do the right thing?"

"Sometimes I do, but there isn't any reason for our leader to do so now. It's getting close to the time we're going to start. I'm guessing our ceremony is much the same as yours. Drinking, singing, aphrodisiacs, sex?"

"Something like that. We do a sacred reading and chants. Do you use spiced rum?"

"Tequila, it's quicker. Also, some pot."

The witches' president shouted. "Witches, the warlocks once again refuse to be reasonable. We must find another field. Follow me."

Lorhon gave a wave goodbye. "Have fun tonight."

"I owe you a drink."

"Next Friday at the Warthog, seven o'clock."

Mijestic tagged with the other witches, hoping the president could find a new field quickly. *What a disaster. The president must be ready to put a curse on all the warlocks.*

A second field was found and the witches quickly gathered firewood and started a fire. They moved around in a circle, chanting and taking drinks of the divine liquid. As they danced around the fire, the aphrodisiacs began to have an effect.

Mijestic and her sisters did their best to stay away from each other, not wanting them to be partners for the later parts of the night. She ate divine food, aphrodisiacs baked into cookies, and more spiced rum. Spells were cast as they danced to the spring ritual, and as the moon rose to its zenith, touching became more prevalent. A female witch stepped between them and grabbed her hand, interrupting Mijestic's planned next move. Mijestic was ready for that obstacle. She sped up and began to swing her partner around. She hoped the action would cause a collision with him, or at least the female witch would lose her grip. It didn't quite work.

The female witch giggled and used her other hand to clutch at Mijestic's robe, slowing them down. A second female witch collided with them and all three fell to the ground. Mijestic was on her back as the other two witches kissed each other and turned their attention to her. One began to tear off her robe as the other planted a breast in her face.

Mijestic gave in. She was too aroused and drunk to resist and began to kiss the skin placed by her lips. The woman on top of her brushed her nipple over Mijestic's lips until she opened her mouth and began to suck. She rolled her tongue over the swollen nipple and wrapped her arms around the woman above her. Hands pulled Mijestic's legs apart while the witch on top planted her other breast for her to work on.

A warm tongue began to lick between her legs. Mijestic wasn't sure if it was a female witch, but whoever it was, was very good at what they were doing. Mijestic sucked on a nipple as a tongue worked its magic between her legs. Her arms were occasionally pinned down by various bodies, and when they were free, she moved them about searching for contact. It seemed whoever positioned her breast on her face was content to switch from one nipple to the other to her mouth. Mijestic was content to suck and keep her legs apart. She freed her hand again, allowing it to wander around, and came across a hairy leg. She realized it had to be a male next to her and slid her hand up to his erection, grabbing on to it like a life line. Mijestic decided it was time to leave the entanglement of female bodies and rolled to where the male body was. It turned out he was medium height, hairy and older than she was. None of that mattered compared to the fact he was a man. She didn't have long before other bodies would try to claim him, but she was determined to win.

Mijestic's mind was in a fog as she straddled him. He reached up to grab her breasts and rolled to put her on the bottom. She held on to his neck and wrapped her legs around him, making sure he wasn't going anywhere. He plunged inside her, and she gasped as her hips tried to lift against him. As she neared a climax, she fantasised it was Lorhon on top of her, and called out the warlock's name when she came.

Mijestic found out magic spells can take away the headache and the ill feeling of a hangover, but they can't give back the energy lost from consuming too much alcohol. She slouched on the couch as her mother handed her a cup of tea.

"Really, Mijestic, the rest of us are up and doing something. There're floors that need washing."

"Sorry. I just want to sleep." She dropped her head back and closed her eyes.

Lucinda put her hands on her hips. "You have until lunch time to have the living room floor cleaned."

Mijestic asked, "Can't we just use a spell to do that?"

"That's not the way we do things here. We don't use magic to get out of work."

As Lucinda left, Mijestic mumbled, "Maybe we should."

Mijestic drank her tea and set out on the task at hand. As she pushed the mop on the wet floor, her mind drifted to Lorhon. *Friday can't come soon enough.*

Mijestic knocked on the door and entered Gwendolyn's bedroom. Her sister was putting on a skirt that left bare thighs from the top of her striped stockings to the hem. Her black lace top showed she declined to wear a bra which meant she had to leave the house without Lucinda seeing her go. Otherwise she would be marched back into her room to complete dressing.

"Where are you off tonight, Gwen?" Mijestic sat on the bed and watched her pick out a pair of black shoes.

"I'm going to meet the gang at Nina's, have a few drinks, and likely go to Raven's Hilltop and party. Want to tag along?"

Mijestic shook her head. The gang consisted of four women, including Nina, and a couple men. Not Mijestic's idea of good odds. The men were both shift changers, and she wasn't sure what they really looked like. Two of the women were wood nymphs and their hunger for sex meant their attention went to women if there weren't enough men. Gwendolyn didn't seem to care who her partner was, as long as they told her she was beautiful. Mijestic didn't mind the occasional female partner, but didn't believe Nina and the gang as a way of eventually getting a man. "No, I'm going over to Accalia's. I suppose we'll hit a bar tonight. Can I ask you something?"

"Sure." Gwendolyn sat on the bed next to her.

"Do you know anything about Lorhon, the warlock?"

"Good looking." She looked up to the ceiling as she thought. "Owns a wicked broom, a real monster to ride. Definitely a bad boy, doesn't care about rules. He's broken a few hearts. Loves them and leaves them. Why do you ask?"

"I've a date with him on Friday. I owe him a drink for his help when I was in the courtyard."

"Mother would have a fit if she found out you were going to date a warlock. What did he do in the courtyard?"

"He reduced the tension of the crotch rope."

"From what I hear, he normally doesn't have any qualms about putting pain to women. He's dangerous and likes to dominate. He's into bondage."

"So, you wouldn't go out with him?"

"Don't be stupid. But you, as my younger and naïve sister, may be over your pretty head in dealing with him."

"It's just a drink."

"Right. Wanna bet you don't end up kissing him?"

Mijestic giggled. "Maybe just a small kiss if he's nice to me."

"Be very careful." She stood. "Now check if mother is in the living room. Otherwise I'll have to sneak out the bedroom window."

Mijestic went over to visit Accalia earlier than planned. With Gwendolyn gone out, that meant if there was any extra chores around the house that needed to be done, Lucinda would assign them to Mijestic. She knew when arriving early or unexpectedly at Richard's house, there was also a possibility of catching Accalia being disciplined.

Mijestic parked her broom at the back of the house and saw Richard through the open door of the tool shed as he worked on a chair. He was superb at woodwork and made furniture he sold on the side. She'd also seen the restraints and other items he made for Accalia.

"Hi, Richard. Is Accalia here?"

He turned to her, taking time before he spoke. "She is. You're here early."

"Yeah, I wanted to talk to her."

"Go ahead, but she's naked and in cuffs."

"Thanks." Mijestic hurried to the house.

She found Accalia in the living room, kneeling with her wrists cuffed behind her back and her ankles cuffed with the same black and red leather restraints. Her matching collar was wide, forcing her head to be held up. A heavy chain went from the collar to the bottom of wall and wasn't long enough to allow her to stand up. She was naked, save for a set of silver nipple clamps and a crotch rope secured around her waist. Pink stripes marked her legs and breasts.

Accalia eyes opened wide on seeing Mijestic. "You're here already?"

"I needed to get out of the house before I had to do more housework. Are you being punished for something?"

"No. Richard just decided to do a session with me. I think he's finished with me, except making me stay in one spot. He says it helps me learn patience. I think it's just to make sure I understand he's in control. By the way, since your time in the courtyard, he figures a crotch rope is a good addition on me."

"Sorry." Mijestic sat on the floor, leaning her back against the side of a chair to face her.

"That's okay. He doesn't make it too tight. I heard that Lady Jacquelyn was incensed that you had more visitors to your punishment than she did. So guess what? She's scheduled for a whipping and a crotch rope sometime next week. She wants to be the star of humiliation."

"She can have that honour. I want to forget it."

"People will remember it all the same. It impressed that warlock."

"Yeah, Lorhon. I'm having a drink with him on Friday. I talked to him at Walpurgis Night."

"Really? How did the rest of the night go?"

"It was a disaster. The president had to give up the field she picked out earlier to the warlocks. Mother said there'll be some serious questions at the next executive meeting. The good news is that I got to meet Lorhon."

"A witch and a warlock? Is that allowed under the Guild rules?"

"Probably not, but we're just meeting for a drink. I owe him one."

"Careful how you pay for that one."

Mijestic listened to Richard come into the house. "Do I need to leave? Give you two some privacy?"

"I don't think so. I gave him a blow job earlier, so he's likely satisfied for a few more hours." She grinned. "You know, I'm sure Richard wouldn't mind having a second submissive tonight. I've another set of cuffs."

"Oh, I don't think so." Mijestic laughed. "I don't see myself as a submissive."

"I didn't see myself that way either until I met Richard. Things change."

"All the same, I'll pass for now." Mijestic looked up at Richard as he entered the living room. She recalled lying on his lap for the spanking he had given her. *Well, there could be something to this sub thing.*

Richard held up a key. "I guess I better let you free so you can get ready."

Accalia replied, "Thank you, Master."

Richard spoke to both women. "Last time there was serious consequences for what happened. I expect you'll be better behaved this time." He crossed his arms. "Or else."

Mijestic nodded. "We'll be good. We're just going to talk, have drinks and dance a bit. Very quiet night. Almost boring."

Richard didn't look convinced.

A werewolf during a full moon was restless, and in Elfwind there were too many full moon nights to make her stay home every time. Thus, he would let Accalia go out with Mijestic rather than have her travel with a wolf pack. The wolf pack would stay out all night, chasing small game in the forest. After one of those nights Accalia would be come home dirty and less obedient.

"Just be careful. The Justiciar would love to have both of you in front of him."

Accalia gave him a kiss. "Don't worry." She hurried off to the bedroom to get dressed.

Richard turned his attention to Mijestic. "Look, I get you like to play the part of a brat. You and Accalia are good friends and like to party. I trust her being around other men, but you..." He pointed a finger at her, "...seem to put her into situations."

Mijestic gave a pout. "I don't mean to get her into any trouble. She's my best friend."

"Let me put it this way. She likes the dangerous part of life and doesn't need much encouragement. All I'm asking is that you try to be the responsible one now and then."

"I can try." She gave him a grin as Accalia entered the room, wearing a short tartan skirt with a white blouse. A black bra could be seen underneath. She had changed her collar to a shiny metal one with a short matching chain attached to the ring in the centre.

Mijestic gave Richard a wave. "We won't be out too late, and I'll try to keep her out of mischief."

Mijestic drove carefully down the streets, not slow, but avoided going over private property or scaring pedestrians. Her memories of her courtyard punishment were still fresh in her mind and she decided she didn't want to draw the attention of the constabulary. Accalia wrapped her arms around Mijestic's waist, trying to keep her balance on the broomstick as it groaned slightly from the additional weight. Mijestic rode the broomstick side saddle, but Accalia had to squeeze her legs around the broom. Her skirt wanted to lift from the wind but she ignored any extra exposure and concentrated on staying upright during the ride.

The Mugs & Jugs tavern, an old wooden building converted from a warehouse to a bar, was lively with a two member band. The female singer tried to sing rock, while the guitar player preferred country, resulting in a unique interpretation of the blues they were supposed to be performing.

The tavern's small dance floor was half filled, or half empty, depending on one's point of view, with several more patrons standing around the perimeter. Mijestic and Accalia sat at a small, high table where they could observe the action, but not bothering to order any drinks. Mijestic did what she usually did in bars, and before long, drinks magically appeared on the table, courtesy of gentlemen who noticed her long legs.

After the waitress brought drinks to their table, the gentlemen were not long in appearing as well. Depending on what they looked like and how they acted, Mijestic and Accalia would talk to them a bit before telling them they were just having a girls' night out. This resulted in a steady stream of drinks from other men wanting to try their luck, and increasingly angry looks from the other women in the bar who didn't appreciate the attention Mijestic and Accalia were receiving.

A tall brunette with a full figure leaned on their table. "How about you two buy your own drinks? Obviously, you didn't spend your money on clothes to cover yourself up."

Mijestic glared at her. "What did you spend your money on? Food?"

"Look, you little bitch witch, why don't you leave before I make you? And take your dog with you."

Mijestic stood and threw her drink in the brunette's face. "Now you have a free drink too."

The brunette grabbed Mijestic's hair and Mijestic responded by slapping her face. The two women tussled, grabbing and pulling at each other as they moved to an open area among the tables. Dancers and other customers turned their attention to the fighting women. In the time honoured tradition of a cat fight, they began to try to tear off each other's clothes. Mijestic could rip open the top of the brunette, sending buttons flying. Her own tank top was pulled off, much to the delight the surrounding crowd, leaving her heaving breasts barely constrained by the black-laced bra. Mijestic kicked off her shoes, finding it difficult to fight with the stilettos on.

The bigger woman continued to be aggressive, pushing at Mijestic. In a sudden motion she pulled at her skirt, tearing it off, spinning Mijestic around. Men and women cheered as she tried to regain her balance.

Mijestic stood only in bra and thong, neither of which was good at covering her body. Another woman may have tried to cover herself up, given up to the inevitable of being stripped naked, or run from the room. Not Mijestic.

When the brunette began to reach for her, Mijestic smiled and pointed to the ceiling. As soon as her opponent looked up, Mijestic delivered a punch to the chin. The woman crumpled to the floor. Cheers erupted from the men and boos from the women.

Mijestic grabbed Accalia's chain and pulled. "I think it's time to go." She was certain the police would be called on this one and it was best she wasn't there when they arrived.

They arrived back early enough that Richard was still up. He rolled his eyes at Mijestic.

"Now what? Did you enter an amateur exotic dance competition?"

Mijestic thought briefly that might be a good excuse to use, then considered getting a caught in a lie wouldn't be good either. Reluctantly she explained about the bar fight.

"... but she started it and called Accalia a dog. What was I supposed to do?"

"I think that both of you created this situation by showing off your legs and flirting with men. If you had bought your own drinks and not flashed your legs, this never would have happened." He sat down on the couch. "I believe a spanking is in order."

Mijestic sighed. "Accalia did nothing wrong. It was just me."

"A commendable statement, and I may reduce your spanking slightly because of it, but Accalia wore a short skirt too. I'm sure she attracted attention as well."

Mijestic remembered Richard had said the next spanking would be done with her naked. She hoped he'd forgotten and slowly eased herself over his lap as Accalia began to undress.

The first few hits were soft, hardly a punishment at all. His hand stroked her back and then unleashed several harder strikes. Mijestic kicked her feet as she bit her lower lip. His hand stroked her back again, this time pausing at her bra strap. With a flick of his fingers the bra became undone. Next, he pulled down her panties, sliding them down to her knees.

Mijestic took a deep breath, suspecting he was about to deliver the harder part of the spanking.

She was right. He took turns on each cheek, smacking hard and fast. Mijestic yelped. As she kicked her legs, her panties sailed across the room. Mercifully the spanking ended, and his big hand rest on her ass.

"Now remember, I took it easy on you this time. Do you have anything to say?"

"I'm very, very sorry for the trouble I caused." *And I'm very, very horny right now.*

"Good. Now go stand on your toes in the corner with your arms crossed behind your back."

Mijestic stood and put her arms behind her back and headed to the corner. She didn't dare turn around but listened the spanking Accalia received. It didn't sound as severe as the one she received, but she still heard her cry out. Shortly later Accalia was also told to stand in the corner.

Richard left the room and return, going straight to where Mijestic stood. His hands went around her neck and attached a collar, locking it with a padlock. Finally, a leash was added to the collar.

"Come with me."

Mijestic followed Richard, keeping her hands behind her back as he walked over to Accalia, taking her by the leash as well. He led them down the hall to a spare bedroom where a kennel, made of metal screening ran the length along one wall. It was waist high and equal in width. The kennel had two doors, one at the side facing the room and another to the outside wall.

Richard opened the kennel door. "Inside. I'll check with you in the morning."

Mijestic followed Accalia inside. She lay down on her side next to Accalia. Sitting wasn't an option, because of her sore ass.

"Now what happens?"

"We sleep. He'll give us a lecture in the morning. Make us breakfast."

"He spanks hard."

Accalia smiled. "I know, but it feels good too. Thanks for taking care of that bitch. That was a great punch."

"I got a little pissed off at her. What do I do if I've to pee?"

"The other door of the kennel goes outside. It's also caged, but there is a corner where there's an outdoor toilet set up."

Mijestic nodded, touching her leather collar. "He likes a collar on women."

"Yeah. I like wearing one. The collar looks good on you. You should wear one occasionally."

"I'm not the submissive type."

"No? You looked like you enjoyed that spanking and I didn't hear any protest about wearing the collar. We just gotta find you the right man."

Mijestic closed her eyes, wondering if Accalia was right. *Right now though I'll settle for just a man. Hopefully he may want to spank me, too.* She felt Accalia move her arm and a moment later a hand was on her breast, fingers teasing her nipple. Mijestic gave a soft moan of approval as Accalia planted a slow kiss on her lips

Accalia pressed on her shoulder, and Mijestic rolled on her back. A series of kisses started at her ears and moved down to her throat, and to her breasts. The kennel rattled as they shifted position and Accalia stopped. "I forgot how noisy these metal sides can be."

"I think we better finish this another time. If Richard comes in here because of the noise, we may not be able sit for a week."

Accalia kissed her breasts once more and sighed. "You're right. Thank you for looking after me tonight."

"I'll always look out for you." Accalia pressed something in her hand and realized it was the handle of her leash. *So, does this make me a sub to Richard and a mistress to Accalia? This is complicated.*

"I trust you to take care of me when we go out. I'll also do what you want me to do."

Yes, complicated.

Richard kept Accalia and Mijestic naked and collared as they ate breakfast with their leashes secured to the back of the chair.

As Accalia predicted, he lectured them again about proper behaviour when going out. After they washed the dishes and cleaned the kitchen, they were allowed to get dressed. Mijestic borrowed a skirt and top from Accalia and waited until Richard removed her collar.

"Think the next time you go out. You can't continue to act like a brat, or there'll be more consequences, and not just from me."

Mijestic nodded, trying to look like she'd learned her lesson. In a way she had, deciding getting into a bar fight because she was leading men on wasn't a good choice on her part. Still, she had a sense of pride of her knockout punch. It was worth losing her clothes for.

EIGHT

There was a certain danger in going over to visit Accalia, Mijestic decided as she headed over to Richard's home two days later. She wanted to visit her best friend, talk and perhaps go out for drinks with her. The visit also meant facing Richard. There was no doubt to Mijestic he enjoyed disciplining her, and she wasn't able to refuse his commands. It might be his voice, his mannerism, or just his physical size. Regardless of the reason her knees became weak when he gazed at her. She had no illusions about her feelings towards him. It was lust, although she didn't have any desire to interfere with Accalia's relationship with him. Mijestic circled around Richard's home. Dusk had fallen, and there was the flicker of yellow light coming through the curtained windows.

If I knock on the door, what are the chances Richard will do something to me? If he has Accalia in restraints, will he do the same to me? I can't keep flying around forever. What do I want to happen?

Slowly the broom spiralled down to the backyard. Mijestic knocked on the backdoor of Richard's home, waited a moment, and opened the door.

"Hello? Accalia? Richard?"

Richard appeared in the kitchen. "Mijestic, do come in."

"I only came to see Accalia, I mean it's nice seeing you too, but I thought she and I could go out for drinks."

He smiled. "I'm sure you can. Afterward."

Mijestic swallowed and followed him to the living room. She looked into the living room, where Accalia sat in an armchair, sewing buttons on a blouse. She looked up smiled.

"Hi, I'll be just a few minutes. I have to finish sewing this first."

"Sewing? You?" Mijestic sat on the couch.

Accalia looked up at the ceiling. "Richard thinks I should repair the clothing I damaged. He's tired of me ripping off my clothing instead of taking it off carefully. He does not understand what's it like when I'm changing states."

Richard spoke, "But I'm betting you'll be wrecking less clothing if you have to repair them."

Accalia grumbled, "Yeah."

Mijestic smiled. She suspected Accalia could reduce how fast she took off her clothing when she changed into a werewolf. It seemed Richard figured that out as well.

Accalia finished with her repairs and received permission from Richard to go out. She hurried to put on her shoes and met Mijestic at the backdoor.

"I can't believe how he knows so much about me."

"It's because he loves you."

Accalia climbed on the back of the broom. "I thought I'd kept some parts of me a secret."

"Richard understands you. You should be happy for that."

The broom sped up and Accalia let out a squeal as they zoomed down the road.

Mijestic went to their favourite bar, The Elephant and Rook. It was quieter than usual, and they didn't have trouble finding a table.

Accalia gave her smile. "I'm glad you came by. I think Richard would have me sewing all night otherwise."

"There could be worse punishments."

"Oh, yes. I've been there before." Accalia took a drink. "Speaking of discipline, Richard is interested in having both of us under his control one evening. I told him that was a possibility."

Mijestic took in a slow breath. "I'm not sure about that. How do you feel about that?"

"I want it to happen."

Mijestic nodded. "Okay. I'll think about it." She pulled her fingers through her hair. "I know you have a special relationship with the werewolf pack, but how come you and Richard aren't engaged?"

"It's complicated. I'm part wolf and I mate for life. One chance to get it right. Richard has offered, but I put him off. I love him, but I need to be sure, very sure."

"I think you and he are perfect together."

"Thanks, sometimes I think so too. Maybe I have to make a decision and take a leap. But not tonight." She grinned.

"Alright. Now let's get drunk."

"Would you like some company?"

Mijestic looked up at Theron standing by their table. She was usually good at spotting handsome men nearby, but the vampire had the uncanny ability of appearing out of nowhere. "Sure. How are you feeling? Accalia told me you had the flu."

In a smooth motion he sat down. "I'm fully recovered, thank you." His eyes, yellow orbs with a flash of red in them, gazed at Accalia. "Your soup seemed to have a miraculous effect on me and I'm in your debt."

Accalia blushed. "It was just something I quickly put together."

"You are a wonderful cook." He turned to Mijestic. "I haven't seen you for a while. I must say you are looking lovely this evening. Life must be treating you well."

Mijestic smiled, trying to avoid looking directly into his eyes. From her experience with Theron, she remembered the hypnotic effect they could have on her and didn't want to have missing hours of the night when she woke up tomorrow. "I'm doing alright."

"Are we celebrating anything tonight, or are you out just to have fun?"

Mijestic picked up her glass. "Actually, to get drunk."

"In that case, I can be of some help." He signalled the waitress to bring another round of drinks.

Vampires were known to have a high metabolism. Mijestic speculated that was part of the ability of having great reflexes, strong muscles and never getting fat. It also, she realized as she watched him throw back another double tequila, gave him the ability to drink an enormous amount of alcohol that would leave most people on the floor.

Her own drinks were slowing her ability to think as she listened to him tell another story.

"It was a great birthday party, but there was too much cake. Vampires don't have much of a sweet tooth, so most of it went uneaten."

Accalia gave a sloppy grin. "Are tooth cavities a vampire's worse fear?"

"Right next to a sunny smile. Do you know what was the worse birthday present I received?"

"Garlic bread?" Accalia ventured.

"No, a sundial."

Mijestic laughed. "An odd gift."

"There are lots of odd things in Elfwind." He lifted his glass. "For example, this tequila."

Mijestic peered at it, forcing her eyes to focus on the gold liquid. "What's odd 'bout it?"

"Well, like almost everything on Elfwind the tequila is made by using magic to make more of it, the spell recipe kept by the bartenders' association."

"That's the same as rye, gin and other liquor."

Theron smiled. "That is true. Now keep in mind I've been around for many years, two hundred and seventy-three to be precise. I hear things. Tequila the drink was originally derived from a plant called agave."

"So?"

"So the agave plant grows nowhere on Elfwind. That begs the question how did they make the first batch of tequila?"

Mijestic tried to figure what he just said. It sounded important but her brain was turning into cotton balls. It hurt to think, and she realized it hurt even if she wasn't thinking. It was time to find her broom and think about tequila another day.

Mijestic tried to keep her broom more or less in the middle of the road as they travelled back to Richard's home. Anyone on the streets, or the sidewalk, was in danger from being hit with her broom. Part of the difficulty was Accalia, who rode behind Mijestic, had trouble keeping her balance. Her shifting weight caused the broom's tail end to zigzag, throwing off Mijestic's ability to travel in a straight line.

After putting a scare into a few pedestrians and horse riders, Mijestic steered them to Richard's home. She fell against Accalia has they tried to open the backdoor. Accalia put her finger to her lips.

"Richard's asleep. We have to be very quiet."

Mijestic nodded as Accalia pulled her by the hand into the kitchen and then down a hallway to a bedroom. Part of Mijestic realized Richard was sleeping in the big oak bed, part of her just didn't see there was anything wrong with her being there. There was also a small conflict in her mind as Accalia helped her remove her clothes, right down to her fabric saving panties, that this wasn't a very good plan. However, by the time synapses in her brain came to that conclusion, she was already undressed. The next logical step, Mijestic decided, was to climb into bed before she passed out.

The first thought in the morning that came wandering into Mijestic's mind was that she was thirsty. The second thought, arriving mere milliseconds later, was that she had a headache. While significant in terms of well-being, those first two thoughts were pushed back by the realization she was spooning a woman. Memories, watered down memories of the night before, came floating back up.

After a few seconds of replaying the night's events she decided nothing furthered happened between her, Accalia and Richard after going to bed. She opened her eyes to the movement at the other side of the bed and watched Richard slide out of bed. He stood and stretched, and Mijestic had a good view of his profile, enough that her headache disappeared for several seconds. He walked around the bed, out of her sight, but heard the rustle of clothes being put on. Seconds later his steps were by her side, and the blanket carefully pulled up to cover her and Accalia's shoulders.

Mijestic decided she was too comfortable and returned to dreamland, determining any hangover would be better with more rest.

The theory proved to be correct when she woke up a second time. She was still cuddled up next to Accalia and moved a hand along her side. She listened to Accalia give a soft moan.

"Good morning."

"Hmm."

"I guess I should get up and get going."

Accalia twisted around reached for her hand. "Stay a bit longer in bed. Richard is probably preparing breakfast already."

"Does he always make breakfast?"

"He likes to get up early and so he makes breakfast. I make dinner." She stretched. "I drank way too much last night, but it was worth it."

"We talked a lot."

"Yeah, we did, and you made me realize something last night. Richard is the one."

"That's great. When are you going to tell him?"

"I dunno. I want him to ask me again. Something with romance involved."

Mijestic giggled. "A werewolf who wants romance."

"Hey, I'm still a girl at heart."

They heard Richard come down the hallway to the bedroom. "Breakfast will be ready in ten minutes. Time to get up."

Mijestic gave him a smile as she made sure the blanket covered her to her neck. She wondered what he thought of her lying almost naked next to Accalia. Her memory flashed back to his nakedness as he got out of bed, and specifically to an extended part of his nakedness.

"Thank you, we'll get up soon."

She waited until he turned away and rolled out of bed. "Breakfast sounds good."

Accalia was slower in getting dressed, but in a few minutes they entered the kitchen together. Mijestic was glad they didn't discuss last night, and in particular how she ended in bed with Accalia and Richard.

Breakfast restored her energy and Mijestic helped wash the dishes. She waited until Accalia left the kitchen and went to thank Richard for making breakfast.

"No problem. Same effort whether it's two or three stomachs."

"Thanks all the same. You know, just between you and me, it might be a good time for you to work how you want to propose to her. I think she's ready, but you didn't hear it from me."

He looked puzzled and was about to say something, but Mijestic turned away.

"Remember, you heard nothing from me."

Mijestic picked out what to wear to the Warthog Tavern. She borrowed Gwendolyn's clothes, a black sheer top with long sleeves and tight skirt that reached midway to her knees. The skirt was longer than she normally wore, but the sides were open with a zigzag string that held the front and back together. As her sister pointed out, the effect was enhanced if underwear wasn't seen underneath. Mijestic left off her panties but decided to wear a low cut bra. *Although he's already seen me naked. What's the point of hiding anything now?*

Mijestic reverted to her sister's trick of leaving through the bedroom window. Her mother would be suspicious why she was borrowing her sister's clothes and might make her put on underwear.

She hadn't been to the Warthog before, knowing it was where warlocks hung out. The bar used dark stone around the exterior and metal doors for an entrance. Brooms were left in front of the bar, the owners knowing no one would dare try to steal them. She left her broom there too, noting most of the brooms were longer with a thicker handle. They were also painted in bright colours, something the Witches' Guild forbade.

She entered the bar, fifteen minutes late. The smell of beer and ozone hit her, and as she made her way, she could tell heads were turning towards her. The furniture looked well worn and the stone floor needed cleaning. Sweet smelling smoke drifted towards her, but she couldn't spot who was using the illegal substance. At the end of the bar two bikini-clad women were dancing to music on elevated plat-forms. The patrons seemed to be an unruly lot, and few whistles were directed towards Mijestic. She spotted Lorhon sitting by himself at a side table with two glasses of ale on it. She made her way to his table, pulling down at her skirt as she sat on the barstool.

"I was wondering if you were going to show."

She surveyed him. He looked on the rough side with a black leather vest over a white t-shirt and the sleeves torn off. "A woman has the right to be as late as she wants." She took a sip of the beer, finding it better than she anticipated.

"Then does the man have the right to make sure she understands that it isn't polite to be late in the future?"

A whiff of ozone hit her and she turned to look at a nearby table. Four men and a woman sat around a table with what looked a new, ice cold pitcher of beer.

"Don't they know using spells is illegal without a permit?"

He sneered. "So who will say anything? No one here cares a rat's ass about those silly laws, anyway."

Mijestic didn't want to get into an argument about the laws she thought were too restrictive. "So this is the place you hang out a lot?"

Lorhon shrugged. "Some. At least warlocks here can do what they want without some nosey cop checking up on us. The cops stay away from here."

"You never get in trouble with the Justiciar?"

He laughed. "No, they only pick on those who can't or won't fight back."

"So why did you help me? Because I couldn't fight back? Or because you didn't want me to be in pain?"

"I don't like the Justiciar, so if I can screw up their discipline sessions, I will. I thought you were being unfairly punished, so I did what none of your family or friends had the guts to do. As far as not seeing you in pain, hell, I would be glad to dish out some punishment to you."

"Really?" She crossed her arms.

"Oh yeah. Such as for being late."

"You have no right."

He leaned on his elbows toward her. "Try being late next time and you'll find out what rights I have."

"What makes you think I'll ever agree to see you again?"

"Tell you what, drink up and let's go somewhere else."

Mijestic frowned as she looked around. "I suppose any place will be better than this dive."

"You may not like it here, but I prefer the term rustic to that of a dive." He grinned. "If you come here a few times, you'll discover its charm."

"Like the dancing girls?"

"Part of the attraction."

She finished her beer, noting he hadn't answered her question why she would see him again. *He sure takes things for granted.* She looked at his face and at his intense gaze was on her. *Damn, he just made my heart skip a beat. What is it about him that makes me want him so much?* "Okay, let's go somewhere else. Preferably a place without women in bikinis."

Lorhon laughed. "You're dressed like that and you complain what other women are wearing? Come on, let's get to you to a place where you'll be safe."

Mijestic followed him outside. The whistles had stopped, and she assumed it was because she was with him. He looked big from behind with broad shoulders. He also wore faded blue jeans and the heavy boots gave him even more height. She glanced at the bar and frowned as one of dancers took off her top. *First date with him and he asks me to meet him at a strip club. Maybe mother was right about him.*

She held her broom as he grabbed his, surprising her with what he rode. Chrome pieces decorated the thick, black handle of a push broom. She heard the low vibration of the powerful broom as he stood next to her.

"Follow me. I know a secluded spot where we can talk." He stood on the head of the broom and held the handle with one hand. It immediately lifted off the ground, doing a slow circle around her as he waited.

Mijestic had her new broom, and although it was fast, she knew she couldn't come close to keeping up with the monster he was riding. "Not too fast. It's hard to sit on this thing side saddle."

He laughed. "Hike up your skirt then and sit on it the right way." He beckoned her with his hand and took off.

She hurried after him, amazed at how quickly he gained height with his broom. She was a little annoyed he had just assumed she would follow him, not even asking where she wanted to go. Still, wherever he was heading had to better than the Warthog.

Lorhon headed toward the downtown area, eventually landing on the roof of an apartment building.

Mijestic landed shortly later and looked around on the flat, gravel surface. "Well, it's secluded but I can't say much about the decor."

Lorhon waved his hand and spoke a few words. Suddenly a cloth-covered table appeared with two chairs. "Do you prefer wine or beer?"

She let out a sigh. "Red wine. You really use a lot of spells. Aren't you concerned about the balance of forces?"

"Balance of forces is just a myth perpetuated by the town council to stop us from using spells. We have the power to make things work for us. I intend to use that power." He spoke a few more words and two glasses and red wine in a decanter appeared on the table.

Mijestic sat and looked out past the hotel. "Nice view."

"So how does a pretty girl like you get in so much trouble with the Justiciar? You don't cast many spells."

"I'm not sure. I usually get in trouble after a few too many drinks, like flying my broom over private property."

"They never bother me with silly stuff like that. If they did, I would hit them with a few nasty spells."

"You're a warlock and can do stuff like that. As a witch, I'm not allowed to cast negative spells."

"And so you end up in the courtyard. Doesn't seem fair, does it?"

"Whatever." She finished her glass of wine. "I've been taught to follow the rules set out by the Witches' Guild." She looked over at his broom. "Where did you get that thing?"

"I made it myself. I came up with a couple of new spells to make it faster."

"You made up new spells? I know no one who does that."

"I made a few errors, but I studied up on how the old masters did spells."

Mijestic began to wonder just what made him tick. He had to be smart to come up with own spells, but he also had a disdain for authority. She finished another glass of wine as he talked about some run-ins he'd had with the police. Unlike her, he was always let off with just a warning. It seemed to Mijestic the police figured out she wouldn't be able to fight back with any spells because she belonged to the Witches' Guild, but he was a different story. It made her upset there were two different standards.

"It's not fair you get away with that stuff. If I do anything wrong, off I go to the Justiciar."

"Hang around with me and they'll leave you alone."

"My mother would have a fit if she found out I was seeing you tonight."

"Are you scared to be alone with me?"

She shook her head.

"You're a big girl. You can make your own decisions on who you want to be with."

You don't know my mother. "Well, I said I'd meet you, so I did."

"You also said you'd buy me a drink. I guess you'll have to see me again to fulfil that obligation."

She smiled. "You wanted to leave before I bought you a drink."

"I didn't think you were entirely comfortable in the Warthog. So you get to name the place we meet next."

Mijestic played with her hair with her fingers. "Pretty sneaky way to get two dates with me."

"If you don't want to see me again, so be it." He leaned back in his chair.

She quickly retorted. "I didn't say that."

"Then name the spot."

"How about the Elephant and Rook?"

He grinned. "Sure, that's where I met you once before."

"That's right, you bought us a drink." She stood. "I better be going. How about next Friday?"

"Let's make it tomorrow instead." He stepped up to her.

"Alright." She breathed heavily as she rested her finger tips on his arms.

Lorhon reached behind her neck with one hand, pulled her close and kissed her. He pressed on her lips until they parted and then released her.

"Don't be late. And wear what your friend was wearing."

Mijestic was puzzled. "Jeans?"

"No, a collar." He climbed on his broom. "See you tomorrow."

Mijestic watched him and his broom disappear. She glanced at where the table was and it had disappeared, along with the chairs and the wine.

Lords of Middle Earth, what have I gotten myself into?

Mijestic wondered if she had enough skills to conjure up a collar. She tried, but ended up with odd looking collars she didn't want to wear. She decided to borrow one from Accalia, wondering how deflect the inevitable questions about why she wanted to wear one.

"You said it looked good on me, so I thought I'd try one on for the night." They stood in Accalia's bedroom where a half dozen collars sat on her dressing room table.

"Yeah, but usually when one wears a collar it's saying I belong to someone. Who do you belong to?"

"No one. I just like the look, that's all."

"Okay. How about this black one? It looks like a choker but has a small lock at the front."

Mijestic pointed at another collar. "I like that one. It looks more like a collar." She pointed at a wide black leather collar embedded with chrome studs. A wide ring sat in the middle of the band.

Accalia nodded. "No doubt anyone wearing one is a sub. You want to use the padlock with it?"

"Might as well do it right." Mijestic hoped her face wasn't as red as she thought it must be.

"Okay. Are you on a date?"

Mijestic hesitated and blurted out the truth. "I'm seeing Lorhon again tonight. He asked me to wear a collar."

Accalia made her lips into an 'O'. "You're sure that's a good idea?"

"No, I don't. But I want to find out."

Accalia nodded. "Be careful. Choosing the right master is very important."

"I'm not choosing a master. It's just a date."

"Right. Then why the collar?"

"Because I want to." Mijestic blushed as she answered. *More like because he told me to.*

Mijestic changed her clothes several times before choosing a leather bustier that used lace strings to hold the front together and a zipper at the back. She decided on stockings with a black seam and pulled on a mini-skirt. She wished she could wear jeans, but her mother believed all female witches should wear a skirt or dress. Some witches wore black pants, but her mother was old fashioned in her beliefs. Under the pain of the hairbrush, Mijestic decided some things were just not worth rebelling against.

She was glad she had plenty of time to meet Lorhon, although she was curious about his assertion he could take measures so she wouldn't be late. She left her bedroom and headed to the front door where her broom was kept.

"Mijestic, where do you think you're going?"

"Out." Her mother would not be satisfied with that answer but Mijestic didn't want to give too much detail on where she was going, and certainly not who she would meet.

"I can see that, but you're going not going anywhere until the kitchen floor is swept."

Mijestic let out a big sigh and hurried to the kitchen.

Lucinda watched her with her hands on her hips as Mijestic quickly cleaned the floor. "Under the table too."

"Yes, Mother."

"Why are you wearing a collar? Have you decided to become a werewolf and a witch?"

"No, I just thought it looked cool. I borrowed it from Accalia."

Lucinda frowned. "You're dressed rather provocatively."

"You don't let me wear pants, and now you don't want me to wear short skirts. I've got to wear something of this century. Not everyone is like Selena."

"The short skirt is fine. It's your top that I was concerned about. You look like your bosom is ready to jump out."

"That's not my fault. I inherited big boobs from you. The floor is clean. I've got to run."

Mijestic hurried to the front door.

"Hold on one minute. Your room is a mess with clothes all over the place." Lucinda pointed towards the bedrooms.

"Mother," Mijestic whined, "I'll be late."

"You rarely gave one whit about being on time before. Clean your room first."

Mijestic stomped to her room, annoyed she didn't close the door when she left. She grabbed her clothes and began to stuff them into her dresser.

"Neatly, or you'll have time for the hairbrush as well."

Mijestic was glad of two things. First, her years of wearing stilettos had trained her how to move quickly even while wearing five-inch heels. Second, her mother had not inquired on who she was meeting. Lucinda claimed she could spot when one of her daughters was lying, and Mijestic didn't want to test that ability now.

Mijestic could finally leave the house, knowing she would be late if she didn't hurry. She shifted her broom into race mode, and that meant lifting her skirt so she could wrap her legs around the handle. Not very lady-like, but she needed speed, not decorum. The broom zoomed down the street, and she used all her skills as a rider to turn corners without sliding off the road. She felt pleased how well she was doing until a cop waved her down, jumping in front of her broom.

She hit the brakes hard, almost sliding off the handle.

The female cop nodded as she looked at her.

"Well, if it isn't Mijestic. Is there a fire we're not aware of?"

"Please, I've a date."

"Right now you've a date with the Justiciar." She began to write out the speeding ticket.

Mijestic figured there was little hope of getting out of the ticket. If it was a male cop, she would've tried to expose more of her top. "Damn. Can't you give me a break? Haven't you ever been late for a date?"

The cop looked at her leg exposed to her hip. "You're dressed like that for a date? Are you meeting him at a strip club?"

"No, I'm meeting Lorhon at the Elephant and Rook."

"Lorhon? The warlock?"

"Yup." Mijestic sighed, not wanting to extend the chit chat.

"You're his girlfriend?"

Mijestic saw she had stopped writing the ticket. "Yes. We get along very well."

The cop closed her notepad. "I'll let you off with a warning this time. Don't let me catch you speeding again."

Surprised, Mijestic took off again. *Different laws for different people. Amazing how the cops fear him. Not fair, but I'll take it this time.*

She hurried into the bar, quickly spotting him near the centre of the room.

Lorhon gave a small frown as she sat at his table. "Late again."

"Sorry. I would've been here earlier, but a cop stopped me for speeding."

"That sounds like you failed to plan ahead."

"I said I was sorry." She snapped back at him.

He pointed a finger at her. "I can make you truly sorry."

"What? Use a spell on me?"

"I was thinking more along the line of my hand on your bare butt."

"Whatever." She turned to give her order to the waitress. When she looked back at him, she noticed a slight smile on his face.

"You're trying to ignore your punishment. What did I tell you last time you were late?"

"You think you've the right to dish out punishment to me? Do you really believe I want to be spanked?"

"I think you're intrigued by it."

"You can think what you want. How about I buy you that drink I owe you and we call it even?" She finished her drink and looked for the server to pay for another round.

Lorhon laughed. "You don't mean that. You enjoy playing on the wild side." He leaned toward her. "I think me and you can have some good times together."

"You and I. If you're entertaining any thoughts of attracting me, learn to speak correctly. I'm not one of your friends at the Warthog."

At first she thought he would laugh at her, but instead he glanced over at the dance floor. "Would the lady like to dance?"

She stood; pleased she'd made a point. She followed him to the small area in front of the band and soon was moving her hips to the music. He was a decent dancer and made a few hand contacts with her. As the song ended he hooked a finger in the ring of her collar, pulled her close and gave her a long kiss. His tongue moved past her parted lips and his hand squeezed her ass.

Mijestic's knees went weak as she wrapped her arms around his neck. When he broke off the kiss, she allowed him to lead her by the hand back to the table.

She noticed her glass was full again and decided not to make a comment on the use of magic. She consumed most of the contents as she tried to understand her feelings for him.

"So how come you're not worried about the balance of nature by using magic?"

She expected a quick, sarcastic reply. Instead, he took a moment before he answered.

"Elfwind itself is magic. It shouldn't exist but it does. When I use magic to create something, all I'm doing is borrowing from another part of Elfwind. The balance is still there." He opened his hand, wiggled his fingers over it as he spoke a few words. Coins suddenly appeared. "What do you think will happen when I spend these coins?"

"I don't know. But you get something for nothing." She frowned. "Eventually there'll be too many coins around Elfwind if you do it too much."

He nodded. "Good point. I don't make too many coins, but what happens is I use these coins to buy stuff, and that merchant uses it to buy stuff. But like normal coins, eventually it will pass through the hands of the government through taxation or fines. But these coins are magic. When the government has them, they disappear." He grinned. "It drives their accountants crazy."

Mijestic smiled. "That's wicked. So they're unaware the coins being magic?" She took a sip of a suddenly refilled glass in front of her.

"Oh, maybe they do. I don't know for sure. I guess Vadith knows and may be amused or annoyed. He has done nothing to stop me though."

"Vadith? Who's he?"

Lorhon looked surprised. "Vadith practically owns Elfwind. He has a lot of power and you don't want to mess with him." He downed his drink in one long swallow. "Why don't we leave this place? Go somewhere a little more private."

She nodded and finished her drink. *I've got to find out more about this Vadith.* "Sure, where do we go to next?"

He took her hand and led her to the exit.

"I think I know of an ideal place."

"Where is that?"

"Why don't we go over to my place?"

She didn't pretend to think his offer over. "Sure."

He jumped on his broom. "Follow me."

Mijestic tried to keep up, but her broom didn't have the power his did. She watched as he circled back behind her, grabbed the front of her broom and pulled it next to his.

She gasped as he accelerated into a sharp climb, taking her higher than her broom was designed to go. The wood handle vibrated as the broom tried to compensate. She squeezed her hands and legs tight, looking down at Elfwind from a new perspective. The streets twisted around each other in an haphazard fashion with roads crisscrossing at irregular intervals. She saw the Great Forest that surrounded the city in all directions. At the edge of town stood the mayor's castle, the silhouette looking imposing with yellow light glowing from the windows. The mayor's home was one of the few that used electric lights. It was one place Mijestic avoided, knowing it was a no-fly zone.

In the twilight she made out the reflection of the Forever Lake and the Continuous River that fed it. She'd heard the Great Forest didn't have an end to it, and from her vantage point, believed it to be true. The Forever Lake had no bottom, and that made sense, as the Continuous River was always feeding it water without the lake rising.

The view was interesting, but she was glad when he took her back down, rocketing to a large stone home at the edge of Elfwind. The three-storey home would have looked like a castle if it had towers on the corners.

He braked rapidly, and as she caught her breath, she looked at the commanding entrance. It spoke that who lived there had power and influence. Some women would have been taken aback after the ride and standing in front of the structure. Not Mijestic.

"Well, it's big, but sure could use some colour. Haven't you heard of flowers?"

"No time for gardening."

"But time for drinking beer? You need to establish priorities."

That earned her a smack on her ass. She gasped and gave him a smile.

He took her arm and guided her to the double door entrance. "I've priorities, but you should be worried what they are right now."

Mijestic wasn't surprised by the interior with high ceilings and an emphasis on dark wood and leather chairs. She was taken aback how bright it was with well-placed lights, but the main room still lacked colour.

"You can tell a woman doesn't live here."

"If one did, do you think I'd invite you in?" He pulled her close.

"I should hope not."

Mijestic felt strong arms against her back, holding her tight. There was something hard pressing against her stomach as she tilted her head back. As he kissed her, she realized the zipper on her bustier being pulled down. His hands slid along her bare back, and when the kiss ended, dropped his head to kiss her neck. Her bustier fell to the floor and his mouth worked down to her breasts, taking his time as he sucked on each nipple. His hands worked at her skirt's closure and it soon dropped to the floor.

She moaned as he dropped to his knees, blowing warm air through her panties as he squeezed her ass. Mijestic rested her hands on his shoulders, enjoying the feel of his muscles. Suddenly, with a quick jerk, he ripped off her panties.

"Hey, those were perfectly good panties." Mijestic pounded at his shoulders.

"Were. If you're going out with me, I prefer you without panties." He stood and stepped over to a closet, returning with several coils of rope. He tossed them on the couch.

"Who says I'm going out with you?" She stared at the rope.

"You're naked in my house. I think that qualifies it."

"What're you going to do with that rope?"

"What do you think I'm going to do?" He kissed her, his hands on her breasts and hips. He pressed against her, pushing her towards the couch.

Mijestic felt his firm member at her stomach, pressing under his jeans. She leaned her head back as he kissed her ears and down her neck. His hands slipped around her arms and to her elbows, pushing them behind her back until her wrists crossed. He closed his hand around them, twisted her around, and pressed her over the arm of the couch.

His other hand reached past her as she faced the cushion and grabbed a rope. Moments later Mijestic's wrists were tied. She pulled against the rope, but found the knot held fast.

Lorhon stood her up, cupping her breasts as he kissed the back of her neck. One hand slipped down between her legs and he pressed a finger pressed inside her.

Mijestic moaned.

"Time for your spanking."

Mijestic nodded weakly as he sat on the couch. She saw the outline of his erection under his jeans, wondering when he would take them off. "Why are you still dressed?" She kicked off her shoes, remembering how they flew when Richard spanked her.

"All in due time." He pulled her over his lap.

The blows were not evenly timed, but each smack was hard when it arrived. She tried to look behind her to see when he would strike, but he seemed to delight in faking a hit occasionally and watching her reaction. He reached between her legs, pressing his fingers around her clitoris. She was wet and annoyed that he knew how aroused she had become. That didn't stop him from continuing her spanking, which was now one of the longest spankings she had ever received. She rocked and twisted her body on his lap to no avail. She cried out for him to stop.

"Are you going to be on time when you meet me from now on?"

"Yes, I promise."

He smacked her bottom again. "Do you also agree I've the right to spank you when I feel it's necessary?"

"That's not fair." She resumed her efforts of kicking her feet and twisting her body.

Lorhon began to repeat the spanking.

"Ow, ow, ow! Okay, okay, you've the right to spank me."

He stopped. "Are you sure you mean that?"

"Yes, I mean it. Please let me go."

His hand stroked her buttocks. "Maybe I should spank you again soon."

"No, not too soon." Mijestic wondered how long he would keep her over his lap. His hand gently massaged her cheeks.

"But not too long." His hand pressed between her legs and a finger pushed inside her, slowly shifting inside her vagina.

Mijestic moaned. She spread her legs, giving in to the rising heat.

He suddenly stopped.

Mijestic moaned. "Why did you stop? Would you decide what you're going to do with me?"

He smacked her ass again. "I don't want you to get too far ahead of me." He helped her to her feet.

Mijestic stared at Lorhon, wanting to show she was still defiant.

"That was manly of you, spanking me with my hands tied until I gave in to you."

He shrugged, took off his vest and shirt. "I thought you deserved the spanking. Do you disagree?"

She recalled Richard telling her she acted like a brat and decided he may have been right. "No." She looked at his chest with well-defined muscles. *It's not as I'd have a choice if he decided to spank me again.*

He raised his eyebrows at her answer. "Good. Drop to your knees." He removed his boots and started on his jeans.

Mijestic took a deep breath and lowered herself with some difficulty with her hands still tied. She stared as his flat stomach as he removed his jeans. She saw his erection under his black underwear, the head straining the elastic waistline. She exhaled as he pulled off the underwear, exposing the thick shaft and the purple head, and saw he had shaved most of his pubic hair.

He stepped forward and stroked her face with his member.

Mijestic stuck out her tongue and licked it as it swept over her lips.

"I want you to take it all of it."

"What if I don't want to?" She licked the length of the shaft.

"Then I'll untie you and send you home."

"I don't want to go home." She opened her mouth wide and took him inside her. Mijestic didn't mind oral sex, as long it was reciprocated. In this case it seemed it would be a one-way street. However, the image of being a sex slave also had its merits, and she decided it was something she wanted to try. He was everything her mother had warned her about. Being controlled by him was just too a delicious opportunity to turn down.

He held on to her hair with one hand as he pushed inside her.

Mijestic was gasping for air when he unexpectedly pulled out.

"Why did you stop?"

Lorhon smiled. "I believe we should go the bedroom now. Stand."

Mijestic looked at his gleaming erection and stood. "You do enjoy ordering me around."

He bent down and lifted her over his shoulder.

"Hey, I can walk."

He patted her bottom with his free hand. "But this is more fun."

Mijestic could only watch the floor as he carried her upstairs and to the bedroom. She looked around the room after she was lowered to the bed. The bedroom used dark wood for furniture with a large four poster bed in the centre of the room. She wasn't impressed with the decor but decided at least the mattress was comfortable.

"It might be more fun if you untied my hands."

"True, but I like the helpless look with your wrists tied."

She sighed. "I'm still wearing a collar. Isn't that submissive enough for you?"

"No." He climbed on top of her.

Mijestic learned that he was heavier than he looked and was very good with his hands and his mouth. She reciprocated his touches, moaning out loud as he played with her. Lorhon took his time entering her and by the time he came, she'd already enjoyed two orgasms.

He stroked her skin as she rested, teasing her nipples until they became firm again.

She smiled with her eyes closed. "That was very nice."

"You liked being tied?"

She nodded.

"Good, because there are a lot of ways to use a rope."

"I'll bet you know most of them."

He untied her wrists, and she curled next to him on the bed, putting her head on his shoulder. She slid her hand over his chest, touching his skin and hair with her fingertips.

"I thought you were going to just make me give you a blow job downstairs, and that would be it."

"Maybe next time."

"So there will be a next time?" She closed her eyes.

"Depends. I want to put my collar on you."

Mijestic was quiet as she thought out an answer. "I don't know.

Wearing your collar could cause some problems, like my mother asking why I was wearing one."

"Tell her the truth."

"I think she would kill me if she knew I was going out with you, let alone wearing your collar. Can't we just hang out together and see how it goes?"

"I'm a more inclined to want it all."

"I'll have to think about it." She took in a deep breath, his scent pleasant to her. "Goodnight," she murmured.

Mijestic woke up alone in the bed and put on her garter and stockings, that she vaguely recalled removing in the middle of the night. She used the bathroom before going downstairs in search of the rest of her clothing. Mijestic heard a pan being used in the kitchen, and after dressing, headed in the direction of the aroma of cooking. Lorhon was preparing breakfast by the stove and she gave him a kiss.

"Good morning. Did you sleep well?" He inquired.

"I did. Do you want help to make breakfast?"

"Can you make scrambled eggs?"

"Sure." She reached for the eggs on the counter.

"I wasn't sure if witches learned how to cook."

Mijestic was glad her mother forced her daughters to learn how to cook and not use magic to prepare food. "I can cook. I'm surprised you do."

"Some things I like to do without magic."

She finished with the eggs and watched as he filled two plates. He carried them to the table where she devoured the food, chatting between bites.

Mijestic thought he appeared to be amused at her appetite and didn't say much to her comments. When she finished eating, she announced she'd decided she had work to do at home. "Thanks for breakfast. It was really good."

"You're welcome. It seemed you were quite hungry." He escorted outside and held out her broom.

Mijestic gave Lorhon a long kiss, hoping he would say something about seeing her tonight. "So, are we going to see each other soon?"

"I think so. How about meeting me at Raegwine Restaurant at seven tomorrow night? We've some things to talk about."

"Okay." She gave him another kiss.

Mijestic jumped on her broom and flew off. She soared high above the town with her legs wrapped tightly around the handle and her skirt pushed high to her hips. The vibration of the wood felt good as she took long curves and loops. If she was any closer to the ground, she would have sat side saddle, especially without panties, but was confident no one could see much at this height.

She thought about the housework awaiting her and decided to visit Accalia first. She didn't normally visit her before noon, but wanted to tell someone about her date with Lorhon. She swooped down toward Richard's home, switching to the side saddle mode as she came lower to the ground. Mijestic leaned her broom outside the backdoor and knocked on the screen door. She paused a moment and opened the door.

"Hello? Accalia?" She stepped into the kitchen and headed to the living room, coming across a bare-chested Richard holding a thin stick. He crossed his arms.

"Mijestic, how nice of you to drop by. We were just about to have tea."

She looked from Richard and to the other end of the room where Accalia, naked and blindfolded, hung by her wrists from the ceiling. Her toes barely touched the floor, and she turned in her direction.

"Hi, Mijestic."

"Oops, it looks like I came at a bad time."

Richard picked up a pair of yellow leather cuffs and advanced to Mijestic. "That depends."

Accalia chimed in, "I think it would be great if Mijestic would join us."

"No, no, no, please. I can come back later." She tried to take a step back but Richard grabbed her wrist and began to wrap the leather cuff around it.

"I don't have time for this. I've housework to do." She watched as he buckled the cuff on her wrist and did the same on her other wrist. "You shouldn't be doing this. I'm not a submissive."

He clipped the cuffs together and attached a rope to them.

"This isn't fair. I just came by to talk to Accalia." She looked up as the rope circled over a hook in the ceiling and her arms were tugged upwards. She hung a few feet from Accalia with her toes just reaching the floor.

Richard blindfolded her, removed her top, skirt and then her shoes.

"Now what are you going to do to me? I've got things to do and just can't be hanging around here."

The answer was a whack with the stick on the back of her thigh. She gasped. Suddenly another hit was on her ass, followed by one on her breast. They weren't hard, but made her jump each time.

Mijestic kept quiet, and after one more smack on the front of her leg, heard Accalia being hit.

Richard alternated between the two women, and Mijestic gave up trying to guess where and when he would strike next.

Mijestic waited quietly. A rope was wrapped around her waist and passed from her back and up between her legs. She groaned as it was secured to her front again. He tested the tightness, causing Mijestic to twist against her cuffs.

"I can make it tighter if you want, Mijestic."

"No, no. This is just fine."

Accalia give out a low moan and then Mijestic heard his footsteps as he left the room.

"Mijestic, he's left for a few minutes. How'd your date go?"

"Fantastic." Mijestic told her a few details, including how he tied her up and spanked her.

"Sounds pretty good."

"It was, except now he wants me to wear his collar."

"That's a big step."

"Yeah, especially if my mother finds out I'm seeing him." She paused. "What're you being punished for?"

"Nothing, really. Richard just likes to have some fun with me."

"How come he's doing the same to me?"

"Because he knew you wanted it too. You didn't object very much or try to get away. I'm betting you're enjoying this very much."

"A little. I'm also a little embarrassed hanging naked in front of him, especially when he tied that crotch rope."

Accalia giggled. "But you liked it, and now you have a chance to have that with Lorhon."

"True, but it's complicated. A witch and a warlock? The Guilds may not approve it, even if my mother does."

"One step at a time. Find out how much he cares about you. Tell him you'll wear his collar when the time is right."

"Okay, that's a good answer."

She heard footsteps enter the room.

Richard spoke. "I guess you'll be staying for brunch."

Mijestic was lowered to the floor, and the rope removed from the cuffs. He took off her blindfold, but left the cuffs and the crotch rope on.

"Don't you wear panties anymore, Mijestic?" Richard inquired as he released Accalia.

"It's a long story. I lost them last night."

"You can tell me at the table."

She gave Richard the short version. "My date got a little excited and ripped them off."

Richard raised his eyebrows as they moved to the table.

Mijestic slowly sat as the pull of the rope between her legs intensified. "There's more. He wants me to wear his collar. I'm not sure if I want to be a sub or a slave."

Richard passed the eggs to her. "There's a difference between the two. Accalia is a sub, a sub I love, protect and control. She isn't just a slave, and you shouldn't accept only being one either. A slave is sometimes merely a tool for whoever owns one."

"Okay, I understand the difference."

"As far as being a sub, I think you like having a master. You enjoyed being tied up a few minutes ago. I could tell by your body's reaction."

Mijestic blushed. "Well, the problem is also my mother wouldn't approve of him. If she finds out about him, out will come the hairbrush." Mijestic surprised herself by finding room for brunch just after eating breakfast. *I better use a spell to make sure all this food doesn't make me fat.*

He laughed. "Accalia's mother still thinks she could do better than to be with me. Maybe it's time you stood up to your mother on who you want to be with."

Mijestic thought about the hairbrush. "You're right, but I had better be sure about him first."

Mijestic returned the collar to Accalia after Richard removed the cuffs and rope. "It seems every time I come over here, I end up naked and tied up."

Accalia laughed, "Is that an observation or a complaint? I think you come over here hoping you'll end up losing your clothes. And end up tied up."

"I'm not sure what I want, although being tied up naked does have certain merits. Maybe Lorhon is the one."

Mijestic tried to sneak into the house by the front door after finding her bedroom window was closed.

"Where've you been, young witch, coming home at this time?"

"I came from Accalia's. We just had brunch."

"There's housework to be done. You've to get the laundry done by lunch time or there'll be consequences."

Mijestic sighed. *So do I try to do the laundry on time and fail or just give up now? Either way I'm getting punished. Unless…*

She hauled the laundry to the well in the backyard and filled a metal tub. She added soap and dumped the clothes into the water. Mijestic took advantage of two things. One, she was far enough away from the house that no one could see what she was doing, and two, the spell for cleaning clothes was one of the few spells she had memorized. She decided if she scrubbed half the laundry herself and used the spell for the other half, her mother wouldn't know. To be on the safe side, she made sure anyone looking outside saw her working hard on the washboard.

Before long, Mijestic carried the clean laundry to the clothesline, hung the items and stepped into the house.

Selena stopped sweeping floor and smiled at Mijestic. "You finished the laundry? There must be magic in the air."

"Oh, hush. Don't you dare tell mother anything."

Selena giggled, "Don't worry. We've all used a bit of help now and then to get the work done. I'm just surprised you know any spells."

"I studied a few." Mijestic crossed her arms. "How come you always wear such heavy clothing? Doesn't it feel too warm and uncomfortable?"

"I'm used to them now."

"I seem to remember at one time you wore more modern clothes."

"That was few years ago."

"What happened? What changed?"

Selena stopped sweeping. "I got hurt by, by someone. He didn't believe in rules and thought the Witches' Guild was silly not to use spells to make life easier. After that I followed the Guild's rules as close as I could."

"Well, you certainly do that. So you weren't always just interested in women?"

"No, I've had my share of men. I just find it easier to get along with women. They're less controlling."

Mijestic nodded. "I suppose so, but I kind of like the guy being in charge."

"You would." Selena gave her a smile.

Mijestic gave her sister a hug, realizing it was a long time since they acted like sisters that cared for each other.

"You're a pretty woman. Witches' Guild rules or not, you should wear something a little more flattering. I'd be glad to lend you some clothes."

Mijestic expected a smart remark from her sister but the answer surprised her.

"Thanks. I'll think about it."

Mijestic went to her bedroom to change, deciding wearing same clothes two days in a row was an absolute no no.

Gwendolyn entered the room as she was taking off her bustier.

"Hey, how did your date go?"

"Pretty good. I'm going to see him again."

"Be careful. He's devious about getting what he wants." Gwendolyn sat on the edge of the bed.

"Did you go out with him long?" Mijestic turned to look at her sister. "You seem to know a lot about him."

Gwendolyn shrugged. "A few dates. I mean it about being careful. He takes what he wants."

"That's okay. I'm getting what I want too." Mijestic took off her skirt and began to select new clothes from her closet. "How come you stopped seeing him?"

"He wasn't ready to settle down. He might never will be. Anyway, we had fun, but also a few arguments. I guess we left on good enough terms." She grinned.

"What's funny?"

Gwendolyn giggled, "After we broke up, I put a spell on his broom to make it pink."

Mijestic laughed. "He must have been furious. What did he do?"

"Nothing. I guess he just accepted it as a joke."

Mijestic mused that wasn't like him.

Gwendolyn asked, "How did you get those red marks on your body?"

"Richard. I interrupted a session with Accalia and the next thing Richard had my wrists tied to the ceiling. He used a thin stick on us."

"Really? You were naked too?"

Mijestic blushed. "Yes, and blindfolded."

"Cool. That would've neat to watch. Does he discipline you often?"

Mijestic thought a moment. "No, just a bit more lately."

"As long as you're having fun. I assume Accalia is okay with his attention to you?"

"Yeah, I think she enjoys company when she's being punished." Mijestic held up two items from her closet. "Okay, which looks better? The black tank top or the black blouse?"

Mijestic planned to stay home for a change, and after dinner, to the surprise of everyone, helped clear away the dishes.

Lucinda thanked her for the help, but was suspicious of her motives. "It's a nice change for you to help, but did something happen that I should know about?"

"No, nothing happened. Well, I was told I act like a brat sometimes. I guess I should be a bit more responsible. That's it. No big deal."

Selena giggled. "Maybe you're finally growing up. A few years late, but you're getting there."

"Selena!" Lucinda held up a finger at her that immediately put the end to the giggles.

Mijestic stuck her tongue out at her sister.

Lucinda left the kitchen with a warning. "Put away the dishes and I don't want to hear about any trouble from you two. Or else."

After she left the kitchen, Selena gave Mijestic a grin.

Mijestic returned the grin. "I guess mother worries about us getting along."

"We may fight sometimes, but you're still my sister."

"Yeah, that'll never change."

"So, who told you were acting like a brat and how did that change how you act?"

Mijestic sighed. "Well, actually it was two different men. And both of them gave me a spanking. It hurt."

Selena laughed. "I wish I was there to watch that. Bare butt?"

"Yes. Naked, if you want to know."

"You do get around." She gave Mijestic a smack on her ass. "Can you tell me who the men were?"

Mijestic slowly answered. "One of them was Richard."

"Ah, the werewolf's master. I suspected he had a firm hand."

"He does. I don't want to be in his bad books, that's for sure."

Selena put away the last plate. "Hey, would you like to go out for a drink? We could ask Gwen if she wants to come along."

Mijestic nodded. "I can't remember the last time we went out together. It's a deal, if you agree to wear something other than what Grandma would find appropriate."

Selena laughed. "So I'm old fashioned."

"Old fashioned? More like old century."

After Gwendolyn agreed to accompany them, Selena inspected Mijestic's closet. She determined that as risqué Mijestic's wardrobe was, it was still more conservative than Gwendolyn's.

The three girls, much to their mother's surprise, flew off on brooms together. They choose a small bar, The Brewhouse, took a corner table and began to talk. All three talked at the same time while listening to the other two. Any man listening left with a severe headache.

One brave man approached their table to see if there was any possibility of getting past the introduction stage. Selena smiled sweetly as she stroked his arm with her finger nails.

"You know, we do have something in common." She looked up to his eyes and smiled.

"What's that?" He grinned with hope.

"We both like women."

His expression changed to a blank expression and then he laughed.

"Can't win them all. Have a good evening."

After he left Gwendolyn laughed. "Well, I haven't heard that line before."

A few minutes later a pitcher of beer with three glasses arrived at their table.

Mijestic poured the beer into the glasses. "He was a good sport."

Selena smiled as she took her glass. "He was cute, but not my type."

Gwendolyn raised her eyebrows. "But maybe he was at one time. Maybe again?"

Selena shook her head. "Gwen, I've travelled that road and I'm not looking back."

"I'm not saying to look back. Look forward. Cute guy. Buys you a drink?"

Selena laughed. "Okay, okay. I know what you're leading up to. I'm not saying never, but I'm happy where I am now."

Mijestic raised her glass. "To men who buy ladies drinks."

Gwendolyn took a drink. "I'll second that."

Selena nodded, remembering the past. "Men are good for some things." She smiled. "And I'm not talking about just buying drinks."

Mijestic swallowed her drink. "Selena, you're more complicated than I guessed."

Selena took a drink and looked at Mijestic. "I've a confession to make to you. I hope you won't stay mad at me, but it was me who used a spell to put that pimple on your nose. I'm sorry I did it."

"Well, I guess no harm came from it. Were you mad at me for something?"

"I thought you were lazy, going out too much and acting totally irresponsible. So I decided to do something nasty. I was wrong to do it."

"You wrong to do it, but you were right about how I was acting. I forgive you." She smiled, "I'll bet you never got a permit to cast that spell."

"No, permits are silly." She smiled. "You won't tell mother, will you?"

Mijestic shook her head. "We all have secrets to keep, especially from her. She will wear out that hairbrush one of these days."

Gwendolyn giggled. "Likely on your behind. You have a penchant for getting into trouble."

Mijestic frowned. "I prefer to think of it as being misunderstood."

Mijestic woke up with a slight hangover, not enough to use a spell to eliminate the effects, but enough to slow her down. She saw Selena reading the Book of Spells, Potions and Curses in the living room and greeted her.

"What are you up to?" She noticed Selena was still wearing her skirt and top.

"I'm going over a couple of spells on how to make clothes. I like some of your stuff, but I need it to fit better. My bust is smaller than yours."

Mijestic nodded. She had made some clothes herself by using a copying spell, but wasn't good at making original clothes that would fit properly. "I sometimes get Claire, the dressmaker, to help me. She's good at adding detail."

"Hmm, that's an idea. Claire and I get along very well."

Mijestic suddenly realized why Claire was so insistent on taking lots of exact measurements while she was undressed. "You've nice legs. Get some short skirts, and for crying out loud, shoes that don't look like they're used to kick down doors."

Selena grinned. "Yeah, I guess it's time for a change."

NINE

Mijestic wore a dress for her dinner with Lorhon. Unlike her skirts, the dress was long with one side held together with a wide zipper that could open at either the top or the bottom. The figure clinging dress was shoulder-less and featured a low back. It made dressing simple, one small pointed hat, one dress, one pair of panties and one pair of ankle breaking shoes.

When she emerged from her bedroom, Gwendolyn gave her a whistle.

"Must be a hot date." Selena added.

"Thanks. Dinner is at Raegwine Restaurant, so I thought I'd dress up."

Lucinda nodded her approval, but voiced a tone of caution. "Don't let whoever you're meeting take advantage of you.

"I won't." She opened the front door.

Gwendolyn gave her a hug and whispered, "Ask him what he did with his pink broom."

Mijestic laughed and jumped on her broom, driving slowly as she made her way downtown.

The Raegwine Restaurant was located in a modern fifty-seven-year-old building. She pulled open the heavy double door and breathed in the smell of cooked food. She walked up to the front counter as her eyes adjusted to the dim light. The hostess took her name, and without the smile ever leaving her face, announced Lorhon was already sitting at a table. She led Mijestic to the table with a starched white cloth and glittering silverware. Lorhon stood, looking very different from his usual casual dress. This time he was clean shaven and wore a black suit with a white shirt and a black tie.

Mijestic smiled at Lorhon as she sat, not noticing the hostess continued her false grin.

"You're late."

Mijestic rolled her eyes. "Oh, come on. Of course I'm a few minutes late. Surely you don't expect me to be waiting for you?"

"No, I was early so you wouldn't have to wait."

"Big deal, so you acted like a gentleman. How was I to guess that?"

"I've never been late before. But you make a habit of it."

"All right, so I'm late. What's the big deal? You certainly can't spank me here in the restaurant."

"Don't be so sure." He smiled a wicked smile. "But perhaps later, in a more convenient location." He paused. "Are you wearing underwear?"

"I am. Not a bra, as if it's any of your business."

"Take off your panties."

"What? You want me to go to the washroom and take them off?"

He shook his head, leaned back in his chair, and grinned. "Here. At the table."

"Seriously?"

He nodded. "I don't believe you want risk disobeying my order."

Mijestic considered her options. *If I refuse, he'll punish me. Likely a spanking right here in the restaurant. So it's obeying him or I break up with him right now, and that's not going to happen.*

She reached to the bottom of her dress and pulled up on the zipper until it reached her waist. She stopped and waited until the waiter poured water and took their order for a bottle of wine. Then she lifted her bottom and pushed her panties down. When they reached her knees, she let them slide to her ankles and bent down to remove them.

"Okay, they're off."

"Pass them to me."

Mijestic made a show of sighing and gave them to him. She reached for her zipper to pull it down.

He casually folded the panties and put them in his pocket. "I want you to leave your dress open where it is now."

"I guess you're the boss." She took her fingers away from the zipper, immediately regretting her words.

"Good you understand that. Let's order dinner."

Mijestic picked out a soup, salad and an entrée. She took a drink of her wine. "About you being the boss. I didn't really say that to mean I've decided to wear your collar. Tonight I'll obey you, but we haven't reached the point where I'm your sub."

"I think you know how I'll treat you, not much different from I do now. So what's holding you back?"

"You have to earn my trust first."

"I'll do my best, but is there something specific that's bothering you?"

"You need to understand my best friend is Accalia, and she is a sub to Richard. When I visit her, I find that I cannot refuse his commands. Even if I was wearing your collar, I would want to obey him. Is that going to be a problem?"

Lorhon frowned. After a moment of silence he replied. "I suppose I can live with that, as long as you're honest with me what transpires when you go over there." He smiled. "It would make a double date very interesting."

Mijestic grinned, "Yes, it would. The other thing is, before I'd consider wearing your collar, is that you meet my family. So far, I haven't told my mother about you, but she'd have a fit if she knew. I think if you were to meet her, it would help her understand what I see in you."

"I'm not sure meeting your family is a good idea. They may have a prejudice against me."

"Look, the Witches' Guild will not be very happy about my association with a warlock. If they find out I've a relationship with you, they may kick me out of the Guild. That's a risk I'm taking going out with you and you don't want to even meet my family?" She put down her fork and crossed her arms.

"Point taken. I'll meet with your family, but I warn you there may be trouble, so let's discuss the right time later."

"Okay." She resumed eating.

"In the meantime, I expect you to obey me."

She slowly swallowed her food. "I do already, don't I?"

"Except for being on time."

Mijestic gave a pout. "A girl needs some leeway there. I don't think I should be punished for being a few minutes late, otherwise that's far too many spankings."

Lorhon looked up at the ceiling. "I can see there are some things you'll never learn." He looked back at her and smiled. "But the rest of you is damn near perfect."

Mijestic grinned. She decided this was the right time to use the ladies room and walked across the room. Heads turned at the sight of the witch with long legs and her dress open to her hip. An elderly man began to choke on his food. A matron gave her a smile. A young woman glared at her. The bartender poured whiskey on the counter, missing the glass. A waiter stumbled, causing his tray of dishes to crash.

The room was filled with whispers that stopped when the ladies room door opened again. Mijestic's return walk caught everyone's attention again, but her audience was prepared and the damage was much less pronounced. Mijestic took it all in stride. After being tied up naked in the courtyard, this was a much more reserved exhibition.

Her walk improved their waiter's attention at their table. He quickly moved to help her sit and drape the napkin on her bare thigh.

"Can I ask you something about my sister?"

"Your sister?" His eyes narrowed.

"Gwen. Don't pretend you don't remember her."

"Of course. Gwen. What about her?"

"She said she turned your broom pink after you broke up. She also said you did nothing to her afterwards. That doesn't sound like you."

"I can't be nice?"

She shook her head. "Not likely."

He gave a small smile. "I put a spell on her so she would find underwear uncomfortable."

Mijestic jaw dropped and then she recovered. "That explains a lot of what she wears. You better remove that spell. This is my sister!"

"Okay, but she hardly noticed it when I added the spell. It could be she just likes to dress that way."

"Don't talk about my sister like that. Remove that spell."

"All right. Shall we order desert?"

"Chocolate. I have a craving for chocolate right now."

After dinner he escorted her to where the brooms were parked by the entrance.

"Let's go to the roof." He waved his fingers at the top the building.

Mijestic followed him to the top of the three story building. His broom climbed vertically while she had to make a curved approach to the top.

When she landed, Lorhon put his arms around her and gave her a kiss.

"Did you enjoy dinner?"

"Yes. Thank you, it was very nice."

His hand tugged upward at her zipper. "Have you ever taken a broom ride naked?"

"No, that's illegal, and I'd end up having to report to the Justiciar." She put her arms around his neck.

He pulled up the zipper higher. "Have you ever wanted to?"

"Yes, but I can't risk it." She kissed him.

He moved up the zipper again. "No one would know."

"You mustn't."

"Too late to stop now." He finished sliding the zipper, and the dress fell to her feet.

"I can see that. You're going to make me ride naked." She gave him a smile. "You cause me to do bad things."

He scooped up her dress. "Meet you at my place."

Mijestic stood naked, except for her height supplying shoes, on the roof top. She watched him zoom off. It wasn't how she envisioned the evening would go. She straddled her broom and took off, climbing as high as she could hoping no one would recognize her. The wood handle vibrated between her legs and wondered if she could make use of that effect at another time and far away from invasive eyes.

She landed at Lorhon's home and entered the front door. "I'm here. Can I have my dress back?"

He called from the living room. "No, not until I decide so."

She entered the living room with her hands on her hips. "That's not very nice." She looked at him sitting on the couch. "I guess I should've expected something like this from you." She walked over to him. "Was this planned?"

"Planned?"

"Getting me naked and riding on the broom."

"No, that was just an inspired moment."

Mijestic nodded. "Now, do you have another inspired moment coming up?" She slid over his lap. "I've been a bad girl." She twisted back to look as his hand rested on her bare butt. "A very bad girl."

His hand rose and came down, smacking her cheek hard. He then repeated the action, alternating between sides.

Mijestic made her hands into fists and called out, "Oh! Oh! Oh!" Her feet kicked, and she rocked her hips against him.

He continued the spanking, turning her buttocks a bright red. Mijestic didn't ask him to stop, even though heat shot through her backside. She moaned and waved her hands in front of her.

"Have you had enough?"

"That's for you to decide." She gasped.

He smacked her cheeks several times again.

"Okay, I think I've had enough. I'm sufficiently punished. I'm no longer a bad girl."

"Really? I thought I got decide that." He spanked her again.

"Yes, well, that was before my ass got so sore." She reached back and rubbed her ass. "Oh, it feels warm."

He gave her ass another softer hit, waited a moment and struck again.

Mijestic took a deep breath, deciding that she might as well try to enjoy the moment. The pain was there, but the pleasure was there too. *I do like lying naked over the lap of a man in a suit.*

Lorhon stopped and helped her sit on the couch.

"Ow. That really hurt."

"So why did you want me to spank you?"

"I wanted to find out if you'd stop before you hurt me too much."

"Did I pass your test?" He smiled.

"You did."

"Now let's go to phase two."

"Phase two?"

Phase two turned out to be ropes. Specifically, her hands tied behind her back and her ankles crossed over and secured together.

Mijestic rested on her side on the floor, her body facing towards Lorhon as he drank wine on the couch. She wiggled slightly against her bonds and relaxed, aware with her legs parted he could see how aroused she was. "Pretty good tie."

"You look good that way. A gag would be a nice touch."

Mijestic guessed almost any answer, yes or no, would cause the gag being applied, except for one. "It's hard to give you a blow job if I'm gagged."

He raised his eyebrows. "True." He stood and began to remove his clothes.

She found it interesting to watch him undress. Most men would tear off their clothes as fast as possible with an offer of a blow job from her. Lorhon undressed in a slow and deliberate fashion. He didn't stop to fold his clothes, but didn't just toss them either. She saw his erection under his boxer shorts and licked her lips as she rolled to a kneeling position.

"Are you sure you don't want my hands free for this?"

He pulled down his shorts and stepped in front of her. "I think you can do a fine job just the way you are."

She licked his shaft before slipping her lips over the head. She felt his hands on her head, not pushing or pulling it, but helping to guide her. He let her take her time to get used to him, easing him inside. She took in a deep breath, taking in his scent. She tasted him, felt his heat and heard his groan of pleasure. She worked on him, sliding him in and out, playing her tongue along the shaft. Suddenly a pulse raced along his member and his hands released her head.

Mijestic decided that was permission she could pull back. She gasped for air as she stared at the gleaming erection, still releasing fluid from the head as it dripped down on her chest. She watched it as it shrank, and she fell back on her heels.

"Did I please you, sir?" She spoke with her most demur voice, trying to keep from grinning.

He walked behind her and undid her wrists and her ankles. "Do I detect a bit of a brat in that voice?"

"Oh no, sir. None whatsoever."

"Good, because I have corrective measures available."

"Yes, sir." She stood. "May I use the washroom?"

He nodded. "Then go the drawing room." He pointed to a hallway.

Mijestic combed her hair in the bathroom mirror, pleased with how the evening had gone. She thought how Lorhon claimed he was a warlock, and by extension, ignored rules of society. But he had stopped spanking her before the pain became too severe and allowed her to set the pace his blow job. He hid it, but there was a civilized man under his bad boy exterior. *A bit of the best of both worlds.*

She entered the drawing room where he sat in an armchair. He had pulled on a pair of jeans and a t-shirt.

"You got dressed. Does that mean I can put on my dress?"

"No. You can wear your shoes. They make your walk more interesting, but you're staying naked."

"That's not fair, is it?"

"I'm a warlock. Fair doesn't count with me."

She smiled. *Tough talk.* "Then I shall remain naked." She looked around the large room with stone walls, dark wood flooring, a fireplace set along one wall and French doors leading to a garden along another wall. The furniture, consisting of four armchairs and a coffee table, were all positioned near one end where the fireplace stood. Two of the walls had various hooks, rings, shelves, chains and various items hanging along the length. It didn't surprise her he had a room dedicated to what she presumed was for discipline.

"Is this what will happen to me tonight?" She gestured at the walls.

"Not tonight." He placed a silver collar, encrusted with gems, on the table. He looked at her.

Mijestic sat and picked up the wide collar. It had a ring at the front with a closure that could be secured with a lock.

"It's beautiful."

"Want to try it on?"

She turned the collar in her fingertips. "It's tempting, but no. If I put this on, I may not be able to take it off. I told you my requirements earlier before I'll become your sub."

"Trust, accepting Accalia and Richard's relationship with you and meeting your family. How am I on the trust issue?"

"Good, actually. I hope you've accepted my situation with Accalia and Richard."

"The four of us should sit down and talk. A sub with two masters is unusual."

"You're not my master yet."

He nodded. "I stand corrected."

Mijestic put down the collar and removed her shoes. "My feet are getting sore and I suspect I'm not going home tonight."

"Let me show you the room."

Mijestic followed him as he pointed out devices on the wall. It seemed to her most of the hooks and rings were designed to hold someone spread eagle on the wall. She stared at a flogger and multi-strand whips. *That looks like it could hurt.*

"Let's go upstairs."

Mijestic nodded. As she he led her by her the arm, she glanced back at the wall with the four rings placed in an X. Her inward breath shuddered.

She entered the bedroom and rolled on her back. "Are you going to tie me up?"

"Do you want me to?"

Mijestic hesitated before whispering out the truth. "Yes."

Lorhon took a length of rope and tied her wrists together that he secured to the centre of the headboard. He used two more ropes to tie her ankles to the bottom corners of the bed.

Mijestic licked her lips as she watched him undress. *It's going to be a good night.*

She watched as Lorhon approached the bed, his cock full with dark blue veins standing out from the crimson skin. His hand touched her face and traced his fingers along her jaw, to her ear and down her neck. He stopped at her breast, squeezing it and then pinching her already aching nipples. She moaned.

Lorhon straddled her, sliding his erection along her skin and on her beasts. She enjoyed the sensation of his hot member on her breasts and nipples, then up to her face, over her eyes and forehead. She parted her lips and licked them, anticipating. His testicles touched her mouth, and she licked at them, waiting for his cock. He seemed to be teasing her as it touched her cheeks under her chin. A trace of wetness was left on her skin. She opened her mouth wider, and the head slipped inside to rest on her tongue. She closed her lips around the shaft, tasting him as he held still. Slowly he pushed inside, deeper and deeper, a fraction at a time. Then he pulled out, allowing her to take gasps of air.

She felt his testicles on her lips again and she opened her mouth wide to accommodate them as he dipped inside. Carefully she licked at the twin shapes as his cock lay across her face.

He pulled away, and his mouth pressed on her nipples, sucking hard on one as he gripped the other breast in his hand. She felt pain and electric excitement at the same time. He switched breasts, again producing the pain and pleasure. Mijestic pulled against her bonds, moaning and groaning louder with each passing moment. Suddenly his tongue was between her legs, licking and pressing just inside. She shook. Her hands became fists and her back arched. She cried out, and he stopped.

He pushed his erection at her open mouth. Slowly he inserted his whole length into her, her tongue exposed to the pulsing heat. He paused and pulled out.

"Sometimes you will understand the phrase the pleasure is all mine. Do you understand that?"

"Yes, Master Lorhon."

"Good."

He touched her lips with the head of his shaft and she spread her jaws again. He halted with the head resting on the tip of her tongue. "Fortunately for you, this isn't one of those times."

He changed position again and placed himself between her legs. He slipped inside her wetness.

She only knew of the rhythmic pounding inside her and then the universe opened up to her as a billion stars.

Mijestic vaguely remembered being untied, but not having the energy to move. He was next to her in bed and she smiled.

"Master Lorhon, I'm a content woman right now. I want to keep this moment forever."

TEN

Mijestic woke up in bed, sliding her arms and legs around with her eyes closed. They failed to contact Lorhon and she opened her eyes. She yawned and rolled to the edge of the bed.

He sure doesn't seem to need much sleep.

She planted her feet on the floor, yawned again and made her way first to the washroom and then downstairs where the smell of food cooking drew her to the kitchen.

She looked at him, wearing black jeans and a torn t-shirt, working a pan with scrambled eggs.

"How come you don't use magic to make breakfast?"

"Some things I do because I find them relaxing." He looked at her and returned his attention to the stove.

"Fair enough. Do you suppose I could have my dress back now?"

"No."

She opened her mouth to say something, but a smart retort wasn't available. She walked over to the kitchen table where utensils were placed and sat. "Men."

Lorhon carried two plates of food and placed one in front of her. "Breakfast is served. I hope you like it."

"A man serving me food is always nice." She looked at him. "How long are you going to keep me naked? I need to go home sometime."

"All in due time. Eat first."

Mijestic ate, finding breakfast as good as she could've prepared. After finishing she took the plates to the sink, preparing to wash them.

"They clean themselves."

"Warlocks don't do much work, do they?"

"We spend our time on other things."

She turned around and faced him as he sat at the table. "Yeah, like keeping my dress away from me. Haven't you had your fill of seeing me naked?"

"Not by a long shot. But I've your dress in the living room and I won't keep you here if you've got work to do."

"Thanks." She went to the living room and found her dress draped over a chair.

She put on her dress and stared back at him as he watched her. "A little privacy would have been nice."

"Don't confuse me with a gentleman."

"I won't. I assume you're keeping my panties?"

"Why don't you come by here tomorrow morning? I want to show you a lake in the Great Forest."

"Don't you need a permit to travel to the Forever Lake?"

"Not if you're with a warlock, and it's not the Forever Lake."

Mijestic nodded, knowing there was little point in arguing with him about the need of permits. She was surprised there was another lake in the Great Forest.

"Tomorrow then." She kissed him goodbye, already looking forward to the next time she would see him.

———

Home meant work, and she wasn't sure of the response she would get from her mother as she entered the front door. It turned out not to be pleasant.

"Why do I even bother having a bedroom for you when you rarely sleep here?"

"Sorry, Mother."

"Sorry, indeed. I believe I've been lax in enforcing proper behaviour among you girls."

Mijestic tried to think of an excuse to avoid discipline. "I had too much to drink last night and didn't think it was safe flying my broom that way. I did get up early and have breakfast."

Her mother frowned. "So you have a drinking problem now too." She crossed her arms. "You girls go out almost every night, drink, party and then are slow to do any work around the house. This will stop."

"I promise to be home early from now on so I can do more housework."

Lucinda shook her head. "As if I believe that." She called out, "Gwendolyn, Selena. Come here now."

Mijestic groaned, suspecting she would be grounded and her sisters were going to be mad at her for getting their mother upset. Her sisters gave Mijestic a curious look as they entered the living room and stood next to her.

"It has come to my attention that you girls don't understand that responsibilities come before play. Selena, you have changed your clothes to something I expect Mijestic to wear and lately have stayed out late until dawn. Gwendolyn, I'm starting to wonder if you own any underwear at all and I'm tired of you sneaking in and out of the house using your bedroom window. And Mijestic, you stay out later than a tomcat and not much more sense with whom you hang out with."

"Sorry, Mother." The girls replied in unison.

"I believe the hairbrush is overdue. Girls, strip below the waist and bend over."

Mijestic closed her eyes and sighed. She unzipped her dress and bent over, resting her hands on her knees.

Selena mumbled, "So unfair."

Mijestic replied in a low voice. "Join the club." She had sympathy for her sister who was finally going out at night and now being put in the same position as her and Gwen.

"Mijestic, have you stopped wearing panties like Gwendolyn?"

Mijestic thought admitting her date had ordered her to remove them wasn't likely to bring a positive reaction. "I wore them earlier but found they left a panty line on the dress."

Mijestic heard nothing more from Lucinda. There was the rush of the air and the sudden smack on her cheeks. She counted out the strikes on her ass silently, figuring ten was the likely number she would receive. Her mother stopped at six, and Mijestic guessed it was to conserve energy for spanking three daughters instead of just one. She heard Selena cry out once. *Rookie.*

After the spankings, Lucinda announced, "You girls are grounded for going out at night for three days. From now on you will inform me of who you're going out with, and what time you'll be at home. Understood?"

"Yes, Mother." They replied in unison.

Mijestic gave Selena a quick hug as she went to her bedroom. "Don't worry. After a while your bum develops a tougher skin. It doesn't hurt as much."

"I hope so. That really stung. I won't laugh again at you being spanked."

"Can I ask where you've been going out to at night?"

"A couple of girlfriends, Essylt and Liberty, and we have hit some bars, and I stayed overnight at their place." She hesitated and then continued. "We've all had sex with each other at one time or another, no big deal there. But at the bars men have approached us, and both Essylt and Liberty at different times accepted their proposition."

"Did that bother you?"

"A bit, but I understood why. I guess I realize I'm still interested in men too. It was just one son of a bitch that hurt me and I guess I've finally moved on from that. And maybe he wasn't all that evil. I was just young and naïve and thought he had the same feelings for me as I did for him. I learned that lesson."

Mijestic entered her room and put on underwear, a skirt and a top. Before she going to the kitchen to wash the floors, she stopped at Gwendolyn's room.

"So, less bedroom window exits?"

"For a while." She went through her drawer and pulled out a bra and panties. "Mother told me I have to wear underwear around the house at least occasionally."

"Yeah, about that. It turned out after you turned Lorhon's broom pink, he put a spell on you that made wearing underwear uncomfortable."

Gwendolyn put her hands on her hips. "That rotten bastard. I should put a spell on him that gives him an itchy crotch."

"No, let it go. You don't want to trade spells with him. Besides, he agreed to remove the spell."

"I suppose so. Well, let's see if I can now wear this bra all day without going crazy."

Mijestic rolled out of bed earlier than usual, wanting to get her chores done quickly. She was grounded for going out at night, but she could still meet with Lorhon during the daytime. By mid-morning she was changing into a different skirt and top, adding a black bikini underneath. She assumed there might be a beach by the lake and might even go for a swim. She hurried to the front door where Lucinda reminded her she had to be home for dinner.

Her mother eyed her suspiciously at the energy Mijestic was showing in cleaning the house but said nothing.

Mijestic flew to where Lorhon lived, spotting him waiting at the front door. She ran over to him, giving him a hug and a kiss.

"I came over as soon as I could. But I've got to be home for dinner."

"Really?"

"Mother has grounded us girls. Too many late nights I guess."

"I thought you were adults."

"Yes, well, her home. Her rules. She won't let us move out until we're in a relationship."

He shook his head and climbed on his broom. "Witches. So many rules."

She didn't argue and followed him as his broom raced across the outskirts of Elfwind and over the Great Forest. Mijestic had passed over parts over the forest before and even ventured by foot a short distance into it. But she heeded the warnings that anyone who strayed too far into the forest was never seen again. The town council, to protect the citizens, required a permit to enter or fly over the Great Forest.

Mijestic looked for anything strange in the dense forest below. She observed the odd creature, but from above she couldn't be certain what they were. She wondered if there were monsters hiding under the green canopy, waiting for unwary visitors.

They approached the Forever Lake, and she was taken back by its deep blue colour. She wondered where he was planning to land as he crossed the lake and passed beaches. He continued to fly, passing the Forever Lake and deeper into the forest.

Mijestic pushed her broom to go faster, trying to catch up with Lorhon. He noticed her and pointed ahead.

Mijestic saw a glimmer of blue and nodded. It took shape as a small, irregularly shaped elongated lake. It never occurred before to Mijestic there would be more than one lake in the Great Forest, and she wondered what other surprises were ahead.

Lorhon landed first on the beach and rested his broom on the nearby grassy field. Mijestic joined him and walked with him on the beach. The lake looked clear and inviting as she peered into the shallow water. Mijestic knew witches always floated in water and looked forward to swimming in the lake.

"Are we going to go for a swim?"

"Sure. Have you gone swimming before?"

"No, but I'll just move my arms and kick my feet as I float. It sounds simple."

Lorhon laughed. "Well, don't go in the water without me."

Mijestic undressed, neatly folding her skirt and top on the grass. She waited as Lorhon undressed to his shorts and then ran splashing into the water. She dived forward and promptly went under. Mijestic stood up in the waist high water coughing.

Lorhon put his arm around her waist. "Are you okay?"

"I think so. But how come I sank? Witches are supposed to float."

He laughed. "Witches are only people who know spells. You can swim as well as anyone, once you learn how."

"Do I have to use a spell to swim?"

"It wouldn't hurt, but let me help you."

Mijestic did as Lorhon instructed, relaxing her limbs as she rested on her back. She felt his hands behind her head. She took slow even breaths and suddenly his hands were gone. Mijestic looked to the sky, as he stood by her side.

"I'm floating!"

"I guess that means you're a witch after all."

"Can you teach me how to swim now?"

"What time do you have to be home?"

Mijestic rested her head on Lorhon's shoulder as they lay on the grass.

"Did I swim okay?"

"I've seen less splashing from a waterfall, but you did all right for the first time."

She played her fingers on his chest. "So are you up to meeting my family yet?"

"Are you ready to wear my collar?"

"A minor detail has cropped up."

"What's that?"

"I think I'm falling in love with you. Is the feeling mutual?" Mijestic held her breath as she waited for his reply. As a witch she knew there was a spell that would allow her to hold her breath for two hours, but hoped that wasn't the case here. As the silence lingered, she began to regret saying her feelings.

"I don't know, Mijestic. I care for you very much. I want you to live with me, wear my collar and be by my side. Is that love? I'm a warlock and was taught not to consider others in doing what I want to. But that has changed."

"I want to be with you too." She thought about her mother and the Witches' Guild. "I hope we can work things out. How come you brought me here? The beach and lake is nice, but I didn't think warlocks were much for romantic or pretty settings."

"I wanted to show you there is a world beyond Elfwind. You're too tied up in rules and permits to see what else there is. The Great Forest has many lakes, and more rivers than the Continuous River."

"I never knew that."

"The Great Forest also has an end."

She lifted her head and looked at him. "I thought it went on forever."

"No, it stops at a mountain range. I flew there. It took me three days, but I wanted to see what else there was in this world."

"That's amazing." She sat up. "What's past the mountains?"

"I don't know." He smiled. "It could be just more mountains or another forest."

He stood. "I was thinking it might be nice to have a lady come with me when I travel again."

"I would like to be that lady."

Lucinda put down her fork and stared at Mijestic as the family sat eating dinner. "Would mind telling me what happened today that's making you so darn happy? You've had a grin on since you got home."

"I met a man a while back and every time I see him he makes me feel good."

"That's nice, dear. What's his name and what does he look like?"

"He's very good looking and I've asked him to come over next week to meet you."

"So you will not tell me anything until I meet him?"

"I think it's better that way, more of a surprise."

Gwendolyn coughed as she tried to take a drink, receiving a kick from Mijestic.

Lucinda looked at Gwendolyn and at the smiling Mijestic. "I don't like secrets being kept from me. I'll let it go for now, but there'll be a lot of questions to answered later from you and Gwendolyn."

Mijestic swallowed hard. *It's not the questions I'm worried about. But the answers may be painful.*

After dinner was finished, Mijestic offered to wash the dishes. Selena passed her a towel with a quiet comment.

"It's almost as you're trying to make a good impression around here, Mijestic. Is there something I should know?"

"Oh, no. I just enjoy helping out." Mijestic gave her a smile. "Honest."

A knock at the front door drew their attention and Gwendolyn called out.

"Mijestic, Accalia is here."

Mijestic hurried to the living room and where a grinning Accalia held up her left hand with a ring on her finger.

"You're engaged!" She gave her a hug. "Congratulations."

Her sisters and Lucinda soon joined in examining the ring and congratulating Accalia.

Mijestic smiled, glad of her hint to Richard. "Let's have a drink and toast to Accalia and Richard."

Accalia looked at Mijestic, "Did you know Richard would propose? It seems like a coincidence that he asked me just after we talked about it."

Mijestic shook her head. "When would I have time to do that? When I was passed out the other night? I think he was just ready to pop the question."

"Well, I hope you find the right guy soon too."

"I'm working on it." Mijestic looked and saw Gwendolyn frown at her.

Gwendolyn pulled Mijestic by the hand to her bedroom after Accalia left.

"You're going to bring Lorhon to the house? Mother will have a fit you're dating a warlock. What's your plan exactly? Do you have a death wish?"

"He really isn't a bad guy. I'm hoping Mother will see that when she meets him."

"I know what she'll see and it won't be pretty. If I were you, I'd hide the hairbrush first."

"Will you help me when he comes over and smooth things with Mother?"

"No way. I don't want to be punished for what you're doing. Besides, I'm mad at him myself for leaving that spell on me."

"Please, Gwen."

"Don't push it, or I'll give you a spanking myself."

Mijestic gave a pout.

Gwendolyn gave Mijestic a smack on her ass. "You're on your own on this one."

ELEVEN

Mijestic squeezed into a short black dress and decided to visit to Accalia and then Lorhon in the afternoon. She first washed her share of the windows, a task Lucinda decided needed to be done with the arrival of spring. Mijestic was also required to spend at least an hour each day studying spells and potions. All of this meant she wasn't able to leave the house until after lunch, and she still had to be home for dinner.

She hurried out of her bedroom, spotting Gwendolyn in the living room. She gave a smile and waved goodbye. "See you later, Gwen. I like your top. It looks really good on you."

Gwendolyn shook her head. "Quit trying to suck up." She gave up a smile. "Have a good visit with Mr. Wrong."

Accalia gave Mijestic a hug after she entered the back door. "I've missed seeing you."

"I've been grounded. Next couple of days I have to be home for dinner and I can't go out at night." She wasn't surprised at what Accalia was wearing, just a pair of black jeans with black cuffs on her wrists and ankles. She also wore silver nipple clips joined by a thin chain. A thick yellow leather collar completed her outfit.

"That's too bad. Maybe I can come over to your place tonight."

"That would be great. Everyone wants to know the details of the wedding."

"It's complicated. I want you to be my bridesmaid but I need to include someone from my werewolf pack as well. Whichever one I pick, the others will feel snubbed. The location is another matter. Most werewolves get married deep in the forest, but that won't work for us. So I'm doing some planning and trying to work out a compromise that will work for everyone."

"I'm sure it'll all come together. I'll help in any way I can. Just ask."

"Thanks, I know I can count on you."

"I like what you're wearing." Mijestic lifted the chain. "This is pretty. Nice and light."

"Thanks. Richard has decided this week I can wear only one item of clothing when I'm around the house, so I added the nipple clips as jewellery."

Mijestic sat in the living room and related how she was going to introduce Lorhon to her family. "Gwen doesn't think it's a very good idea, but eventually they have to meet him."

"True, but how you introduce him will be critical. Are you going to wear his collar when he comes over?"

"No, Mother will have a fit as it is."

"Likely a good decision. However, Richard said that you're in need of training as a sub."

"Well, I let Lorhon be the boss."

Accalia shook her head. "You don't quite get it. You don't let him be the boss. He takes control. When you wear his collar, you'll understand that better."

"Okay, I guess I see your point."

"Good, because also understand Lorhon will have to discipline you a lot initially. Richard said he'll be happy to teach you some basic sub duties and positions." She gave a grin.

"I'll bet he would."

"Just remember, the master comes first in your thoughts."

"Okay, thanks for the advice."

"Look, I'm serious that you need to learn how to act submissive. It can be a painful set of lessons. I can tell you think all that means is obeying your master, but it's more than that. It's your attitude when he's around, and even when he's not. You should let Richard teach you a few things and you'll be much better prepared for Lorhon."

"All right, I'll think about it. Right now I better chase over to Lorhon's place."

"All right. Have fun."

Mijestic flew over to Lorhon's home, curious about the sub training Accalia talked about. She landed near the front steps of his home and entered.

"I'm here." She called out. She didn't hear a reply and continued into the house. Mijestic entered the hall and into the study, finding him sitting at a loveseat.

"Hi, didn't you hear me?"

Lorhon nodded. "I wanted you to come in here."

"Why? Because of what's in this room?"

"Yes, because if you live with me, you'll be spending some time here." He stared at her.

"Your need to train me, is that it?"

"Yes, are you worried about that?"

Mijestic shrugged. "Does it matter? I accept it as part of being with you."

"Then perhaps you're looking forward to it. However, you have a lot to learn about being a sub."

"If you say so." She looked along the wall. "Anyway, I thought that you could come over for dinner the day after tomorrow."

Lorhon slowly nodded. "If that's what you want."

She smiled. "I do. I think you'll be a big hit."

He kissed her, and his hands wandered over her body. Mijestic sighed as her body became limp in his arms.

"Lorhon, I need to get home. If I'm late for dinner...I'd rather not think about it."

He released her. "Okay, but you're not going to run from me forever." He gave a small pat on her ass. "Eventually I shall get you to stay here."

Mijestic made it home in time for dinner. It involved racing her broom beyond the posted speed limits, but she now had a certain immunity to the police. She burst through the front door just as the food was being placed on the table.

Lucinda frowned. "You're cutting it a bit fine."

"Sorry. It was a long ride to get back here."

Gwendolyn laughed. "How was the other ride?"

Lucinda held up a finger, and the laughter stopped. "Gwendolyn, I do not find that funny and not the humour ladies should be using."

Mijestic sat and gave Gwendolyn a smile. "I saw Accalia and invited her to come over this evening. I hope that's all right."

Lucinda passed the potatoes. "Of course, Accalia is always welcome here."

Selena sighed. "And a good reason why we can't keep any cats around here."

Mijestic replied, "Accalia can't help it that cats won't stay around any place where a werewolf has been. She wouldn't hurt one."

"I've seen a pack of werewolves and they looked like they could devour a horse, let alone a cat."

Mijestic didn't reply. Werewolves had a bad reputation in Elfwind. Most, when in their wolf state, had a poor temperament and a hunger for flesh. The human part of their brain usually kept their desires in check, but there were instances of a lapse of judgement.

Dinner was finished and Mijestic helped clear the table and wash the dishes.

Selena commented on her help. "I don't know who your new beau is, but he sure has managed to get you to do more work around here. I'm looking forward to meeting him."

"I'm sure you'll like him, even if he is a man. Good looking, well-mannered and smart."

"Sounds like a good catch." She put her arm around Mijestic and gave a squeeze. "I'm happy for you. Let's hope he passes mother's qualifications."

"I hope so too." Mijestic thought of how she was going break in the news he was a warlock. "She can be picky about details."

A howling at the door announced Accalia's arrival. Mijestic quickly answered the door, and the wolf bounded in. The wagging tail threatened to knock over a vase and Mijestic pulled on her collar to the centre of the living room. She bent down and gave the wolf a hug.

"It's great to see you again, Accalia."

Selena and Gwendolyn entered the living and said hello. Lucinda looked in from the kitchen and greeted her. "It's so nice you came over. It's been a while since you've been here. She looked at Gwendolyn. "I'm sure Accalia could use some tea and biscuits."

Gwendolyn sighed and went to kitchen to make tea and warm up the biscuits as Accalia began to change into her human form.

Selena sat on the loveseat, watching the wolf change into a woman. She gave a smile as she stared at the naked body kneeling on the floor. "Why don't you sit next to me and tell me what've you been up to lately? I want to hear about your wedding plans."

Mijestic frowned as Accalia slowly stood, looking around the room. She was still dazed from her transformation and accepted the offer to sit down next to Selena. "I'll get you something to wear." She went to her room, but glanced back in time to see Selena's hand on Accalia's leg.

The closet contained mostly tight-fitting clothes, but Mijestic found a loose fitting top that was long enough to be a short dress. By the time she returned to the living room, Selena was holding her hand and eliminated the space between them.

"Here, Accalia. Something for you to wear."

Selena replied. "Oh, she's just with us. We're like family to her. She can stay the way she is."

Mijestic looked at the ceiling and passed the top to Accalia, who stood to put it on.

Selena crossed her arms and pouted.

Mijestic shook her head at Selena. "Accalia, how's Richard doing?" She sat on the couch and smiled as Accalia joined her, curling a leg under her to face Mijestic.

"Good. He's doing some woodwork. Someone has paid him to make a table with chairs."

Gwendolyn brought in a tray with tea and biscuits. "Here are some refreshments. Homemade biscuits, as Mother refuses to let us use magic."

Lucinda sat in an armchair. "Someday you'll thank me I taught you girls how to do things without magic. Magic is not be used to replace doing work we can do ourselves. The balance force of nature has to be respected."

Mijestic had heard that lecture too many times and moved to change the subject by passing the biscuits to Accalia.

"Here, try them. They're very good."

"Thanks, I could eat a horse right now."

Selena took a cup of tea. "What did I tell you?"

The conversation went well and as midnight approached, Accalia announced she had to head home soon. "Richard said midnight, and I know what will happen if I'm late."

Lucinda nodded. "He does make sure you don't get in trouble."

"He does. I was pretty wild before I met him."

"How did you meet him?"

Accalia blushed. "I was digging up his garden. Most humans are scared of wolves, but not him. He marched right up to me as I was digging and grabbed me by my collar. I yelped and growled at him but he just dragged me to the tool shed and threw me in there. He locked the door, trapping me inside for the night. I was so mad, but there wasn't anything I could do. In the morning he hauled me, naked and human, into the house and gave me a lecture. I said I was sorry, and he gave me a t-shirt to wear. He ended up making me breakfast. One thing led to another, but I knew from that day on he was my master."

"So you like him controlling you?"

"Oh yes. I was a real delinquent before and got in so much trouble. Now I wear his collar and respect what my boundaries are. My parents are adjusting to him, and my mother actually told me I was better with him than without him."

Lucinda nodded. "That's something my girls could learn. Of course I'm not sure what man, or woman, would be up for that task."

TWELVE

Mijestic woke up with thoughts of what she needed to do that day. Yesterday's events played over in her mind and she decided she needed to do as Accalia suggested. She wanted to learn how to be submissive for Lorhon, even if that meant asking Richard for help.

She rushed through her required work of studying magic spells, washing the kitchen floor, tidying up her room and cleaning the living room walls. She hurried out the front door, declining to have lunch.

"I'll eat at Accalia's." She called out to her mother, who peered at her with suspicion.

"You spend an awful lot of time there. I hope Richard doesn't start charging you rent."

"I just want to ask for some advice. I'll be back for dinner."

Mijestic climbed on her new broom. She was certain she was going to lose her clothes and chose a loose fitting skirt and a tank top, items that could come off easy. She pushed her broom hard, wanting to feel the acceleration and the wind blowing. She let the skirt float around her hips, not worried about getting in trouble for public exposure any more.

Her broom twisted along the streets and she laughed when she flew just over the heads of young men playing a game of rugby in a schoolyard. The cheers encouraged her to make a second pass, and she lifted her top for good measure.

She was in a good mood when she arrived at Richard's home and knocked on the backdoor.

"Hello?"

Accalia answered the door, wearing only a blue skirt. "Hey, you're just in time for lunch."

"Does Richard allow a submissive in training to eat?"

Accalia took her hand and smiled. "It's good you took my advice and let Richard teach you some lessons. Come, I'll make you a sandwich. You can't learn on an empty stomach."

As Mijestic ate, Accalia explained to Richard that Mijestic agreed she needed to be trained before Lorhon became her master.

"I think he could be rather harsh and Mijestic needs to learn how to behave." Accalia spoke to Richard. "I hope you'll help her."

Richard looked at Mijestic. "I'll be glad to give you some lessons. After you finish eating, strip off your clothes and have Accalia put on cuffs and a collar on you. Then come to the living room."

Mijestic chewed on her sandwich carefully, glad that Accalia would be around for her training.

Mijestic kneeled in the centre of the living room, resting the palms of her hands upward. Her knees were spread apart as Richard circled around her, holding a riding crop in his hand. Across the room, Accalia sat in an armchair, her chin resting on her hands as she stared at Mijestic.

Another strike on her back by Richard caused Mijestic take in a sudden breath.

"Shoulders back." He stood in front of her. "That's better." She focused on his bare chest and his leather pants, leather pants with an obvious bulge.

Mijestic swallowed. "Thank you, Master Richard." Mijestic wondered how many more positions she had to learn. She had gone from standing, to lying prone on the floor with her ass up, to being on her back and now kneeling. Her body tingled from the numerous hits she had received, most of them at the beginning of her training when Richard decided she didn't have the right facial expression.

He grabbed a fistful of her hair and pulled her face to his groin.

She breathed in the scent of leather as his erection pressed against her mouth. Mijestic parted her lips as she sucked in air, his member under his pants radiating warmth to her mouth.

He continued to hold her there for a few seconds before releasing her. "I've placed a thin cane on the floor by the couch. You're to crawl to it and bring it to me by carrying it your mouth. Make sure you shift your hips as you do so. Understand that I'll be using it on you after you bring it to me." He held her chin in the palm of his hand. "I'm telling you this because you need to do this without hesitation, even though there'll be pain for you afterward." He took away his hand. "Go."

Mijestic crawled to the cane, remembering to shift her hips. She took the cane in her mouth, returning to where Richard stood with his arms crossed next to Accalia. She paused at his legs, waiting.

Richard took the cane from her. "Arms in front, ass in the air."

Mijestic slid her hands forward until her breasts rested on the floor, keeping her knees on the floor. She studied the floor as he walked behind her, observing there wasn't a lot of wolf hair lying around. Her mother was finicky about keeping floors clean, and Mijestic found she often inspected floors in other homes, although this time she had a very close look. There was a whistle of air and suddenly the sting of the rod on her ass. Mijestic gasped, but held her position. Several more strikes on her cheeks came, each one burning her skin. She made her hands into fists, waiting for him to stop.

"Very good. You didn't flinch." He stroked her back and ass with the rod. "You've done well and we can stop now if you want. The next part will hurt even more."

Mijestic considered the information. She wasn't eager for more pain, as it was painful. On the other hand, she wanted to learn more what Lorhon might do to her and if she could handle it. Besides, if a werewolf could take it, surely a witch could too.

"I want to continue." She tried to speak in a clear voice, hampered due to the proximately of her face to the floor. She listened to Richard instruct Accalia on how to restrain her and soon found her wrists being attached to chains that hung from ceiling hooks.

Accalia whispered to her, "It hurts at first, but you'll soon get used to it. Don't cry out, or he'll gag you. The neighbours like to complain over every little thing."

Mijestic didn't have a burst of confidence from that revelation, but nodded as Accalia bent down to secure a pole between the ankle cuffs, forcing her legs apart. It didn't help her nerves as Richard walked around her, swinging a flogger in his hand. She looked on the couch, where other whips and devices waited.

"Obedience is the first step." He swung the whip across her back once and continued to walk around her. "But obedience in itself is not sufficient. You must anticipate what has to be done before being told." He struck again, this time on her stomach. "Attitude is also important. You must want to please your master and obey because you want to and not because of fear." He struck again on her back. "You must also realize that your master, for his own reasons, will need to discipline you. This can occur regardless of whether or not you've been obedient."

Mijestic groaned at the whip hit her several times on her back. She breathed deeply through her mouth as Richard whipped her breasts, legs, and continued on her back. She took a deep breath, waiting for him to continue. When he reappeared in front of her, he was naked, with a full erection. That would have normally drawn her complete attention, but he was still holding the whip. He struck again, once between her legs and then across her breasts. Richard tossed the whip on the couch.

"That's it for the first lesson."

The first? She was going to voice that concern but became distracted by Accalia giving Richard oral sex. *Am I supposed to watch this or pretend I don't see it? My goodness, she is good at that. She's tracing his head with her tongue and...Okay, I guess I'm supposed to watch, but I never thought of BDSM as a spectator sport. But should I do or say something, like wow, that was great or nice move? What's the etiquette here? This is worse than an orgy and finding the person to thank afterwards.*

Mijestic waited patiently until they were finished. Accalia removed her from her restraints and whispered to her.

"You did great, no crying out and your body has a hundred strokes on it. Kneel in front of Richard and keep your eyes lowered."

Mijestic did as Accalia suggested. She kneeled in front of Richard who sat relaxed in a chair, trying not to stare at between his legs, failing completely.

"You did well, Mijestic. You took the punishment and acted submissive." He leaned forward and stroked her hair. "I will release you now. You may get dressed now."

Breathing a sigh of relief, Mijestic hurried to get dressed. She thanked Richard and Accalia for their help. "I have to go home, but thanks for preparing me for what I can expect from Lorhon." She gave Accalia a hug and hurried out the door, before Richard determined she needed another lesson.

THIRTEEN

Mijestic paced around the house, sweeping up invisible dirt from the floors and rearranging the cushions on the couch until Lucinda finally told her to sit still.

"Stop it, or I'll find real work for you to do. You're fidgeting more than a vampire in a roomful of crosses."

The chair looked a good place to settle down and Mijestic forced herself to sit. Moments later a knock on the door caused Mijestic to leap to her feet. "I'll get the door," she yelled needlessly.

She swung open the door.

Lorhon stood at the entrance, standing stiffly in a black suit, black shirt and a white tie. He held a bottle of wine. "I had two, but I drank the other before I came here."

Mijestic grinned. "Come in and meet my family."

He stepped past the front entrance and into the living room, where the rest of Mijestic's family waited.

"Everyone, this is Lorhon." She pointed to her sisters and her mother as she introduced them.

Gwendolyn stepped up him. "We've met before." She slapped him hard on his left cheek. "I believe you know what that's for."

Lorhon rubbed his cheek. "I think so."

Selena approached him. "You bastard!" She slapped his right cheek. "I wish you were dead." She slapped him again for good measure.

Lucinda stood in to him. "When you left, I thought I told you I never wanted to see your face here again." She slapped his left cheek and his right cheek.

"My sisters and my mother?" Mijestic slapped Lorhon on his right cheek.

Lorhon stood with two red cheeks. "I suppose I had that coming. Perhaps not all at once, but I can't blame any of you." He stared at the four women glaring at him. "Look, I made mistakes in the past and I'm sorry for that. But I've changed and want to settle down with a woman I care a great deal about. Can we forget the past and look where we are today?"

Mijestic stood with her hands on her hips. "Go to hell. Go directly to hell. Do not go past go. Do not collect two hundred spells."

"Look, let me explain."

"I don't want to hear it. Good bye." She turned her back on him, crying as she ran to the living room. Selena put her arms around, patting her back as Mijestic sobbed on her shoulder.

Lorhon lowered his head and turned around to leave.

Gwendolyn let out a sigh. "Oh crap, what the hell?" She called out to Lorhon. "Wait, don't you dare leave now. Face the music if you truly love her."

Lucinda looked surprised at Gwendolyn.

"Mother, we all went out with him, and we know his attraction. You may not like him now, but he has been good to Mijestic. You saw how Accalia was changed by Richard? Well, I think Mijestic needs a strong man in her life too."

Lucinda nodded and stared to Lorhon. "You should come in and have a talk with us."

Lorhon nodded and returned to the house. He eyed Selena as he made his way to the living room. He choose an armchair, across from Selena, Mijestic and Gwendolyn on the couch and Lucinda in another armchair.

Lucinda spoke. "I think we should listen what we each have to say. Afterward, I'll like to know why Mijestic decided, in Middle Earth's name, to go out with a warlock. A deceitful, cheating, no good, lying one at that."

"Don't forget leaving spells on unsuspecting ladies." Gwendolyn added.

"Or dumping a lady after she falls in love with him." Selena chimed in.

Mijestic spoke. "At least now I know why you didn't want to meet my family."

"I'm sorry for all that." Lorhon spread out his hands. "What would you like me to say?"

"You were supposed to know I was in love with you. Bastard." Selena pouted.

Gwendolyn crossed her arms, "Leaving that spell on me after all that time. Shame on you. Can you guess how many times I had to sneak out of this house through my bedroom window because I couldn't stand wearing underwear?" She noticed how depressed Mijestic looked, slumped on the couch. "However, I must say that since Mijestic has been going out with him, her attitude around here has improved. She helps around the house a lot more. He has a good influence on her."

Lucinda nodded. "That's true." She spoke to Gwendolyn, "Just how long have you known she was going out with him?"

Gwendolyn stuttered her reply, "Ah, I'm not sure exactly. She talked about going out with a mysterious man. Later, ah, I guessed it was Lorhon."

Lucinda nodded. "We'll talk later about this." Lucinda raised her voice, causing her daughters to listen attentively. "The fact remains Lorhon is a warlock. Witches should not be seen in their company according to the Witches' Guild."

Selena frowned. "That's true, Mother. But you went out with him. How's that different for the rest of us?"

"It was different then. The witches and the warlocks had a different understanding than they do today."

Selena raised her eyebrows. "Come on. Different back then? You can't expect us to believe that excuse. The rules for the Guild haven't changed in a hundred years."

Lucinda looked at Mijestic. "All right, I guess we all were attracted to him and paid a price for that. You still love him?"

"Yes." Mijestic looked at Lorhon.

Lucinda spoke to Lorhon. "Do you truly love Mijestic? Or is she just another notch on the bedpost for you?"

"I love her. I don't want to ever lose her."

"Then you two have my blessing. I will forgive your past indiscretions, Lorhon."

Mijestic walked over to sit on Lorhon's lap, tears rolling down her cheeks.

Lucinda frowned. "But the Witches' Guild may not permit a union between a witch and a warlock. You might have to choose between him and being a registered witch."

Lorhon nodded, "I may have a way around that problem. Perhaps if you could arrange a meeting for me with the Guild's president, I could convince her to let us be together."

"All right, I can do that. Now if Gwendolyn would get us each a glass of wine, we can do a proper toast to Mijestic and Lorhon."

Mijestic grinned at the news. "Thank you, Mother."

Lucinda continued. "However, until Lorhon provides my daughter with an engagement ring, she will spend the nights at home."

"Mother!"

"I believe Lorhon will see the urgency in making a commitment if he's sleeping alone. Also, the ring cannot be made by magic. My decision is final."

Mijestic cleaned the kitchen the following morning. She felt happy about Lorhon, but frustrated she had to sleep at home. *It seems I'm getting ordered around by everyone. Mother makes me sleep at home. Then she goes out to talk to the Guild president and Selena orders me to clean the kitchen. I want to go over to talk to Accalia, where Richard can order me around. And Lorhon, he's already giving me orders, like telling me I can't wear any panties this week. It isn't easy having so many people in charge of you.*

Selena came into the kitchen and inspected the floor. Her hands were on her hips. "That's a sloppy job. You need to learn to do a better job for when you don't live here anymore. You don't want to disappoint Lorhon with sloppy housework. Bend over the table."

"But I haven't finished yet."

"The table." Selena pointed at the black, wood kitchen table.

Mijestic dropped the mop handle and bent over the table, resting her hands above her head. She turned her head to watch Selena pull a wooden spoon from a drawer and march toward her.

Selena tugged Mijestic's short leather skirt up to her hips. "No panties? I must give you extra smack for that."

Mijestic felt the burn on her cheeks as each smack pushed her harder against the table. She wasn't surprised she was getting a spanking from Selena. *I think it's her way of saying she loves me and will miss me. I wish she'd find a less painful way of doing that. Ouch, that last hit hurt a bunch.*

"Okay, now do a better job."

Mijestic nodded and pulled down her skirt over her red cheeks. Her ass was sore and the skin tinkling from the ten smacks with the spoon. She took extra care with the mop, knowing Selena was looking for an excuse to punish her again. She wished her mother would come home soon, who would likely allow her to go out.

Gwendolyn came into the kitchen, stepping on the wet floor. "Sorry, I wanted to make some tea."

"Are you and Selena determined to find ways of punishing me?" She looked at the footprints on the floor.

Gwendolyn thought for a moment, looking up at the corner of her eye. "Yeah, pretty much so. Do you know how tough it will be living here after Mother found out what you were doing? She blames us for allowing you to get involved with a warlock. You get to live happily ever after with Lorhon and I'm stuck here doing housework. Yes, you will pay for that."

"Gwen, I did nothing with the intention of hurting you."

"Yeah, well, the result was the same." She patted Mijestic on the ass. "Later."

Mijestic cleaned the kitchen floor and was excited when Lucinda come in the front door. She hurried to the living room.

"Well, what did the president say?"

"Helga was reluctant to meet him, but I convinced her it wouldn't hurt to have a short meeting. So Lorhon will have a chance to keep you in the Guild, but I can't think of anything he can say that will change Guild policies regarding your relationship."

"Thanks all the same. I cleaned the kitchen floor. Can I see Accalia? I'll be back for dinner."

"All right. Say hello to her for me."

Mijestic left before her sisters could interfere and make up a story how disobedient she was to keep her at home.

As usual, Mijestic parked her broom at the backdoor of Richard's home. She knocked once and entered. "Hello? It's me."

Richard looked in from the entrance to the living room from the kitchen. "Hi, Mijestic. Come on in."

"I hope you don't mind I dropped by, but I wanted to tell you and Accalia some good news. My mother has allowed Lorhon and I to stay together."

Mijestic noticed Accalia was kneeling on the floor next to an armchair. She was nude, with her wrists and head inside a polished wood yoke. A short length of black iron chain went between her cuffed ankles. Accalia twisted her body to look at her. She grinned, "That's great news. Are moving in with him now?"

"No, my mother said I can't sleep over at his place until he provides an engagement ring."

"Good for her. I'll bet he'll get one quick."

Mijestic looked at Accalia kneeling on the floor. She looked at Richard, removed her shoes and kneeled next to Accalia with her hands behind her back. She gave a smile to Richard. "Sorry, Master Richard, I should have kneeled right away."

"That is noted. Normally you should be disciplined for that. However, I'll let that go seeing that you were so excited about your news."

"Thank you, Master Richard." She looked at Accalia. "I wanted to ask about when I put on his collar. Do I do that right away, or is there a ceremony I go through? You were already wearing a collar as a werewolf, so was it different for you?"

"A bit different for me, as I was wearing a collar that identified my pack. Our pack uses star shaped studs and a red band in the collar. I usually wear that when I go outside. In the home I have several collars to choose from. I have one collar that conforms to my pack, but was made by Richard to his design. That's my favourite. But before I submitted to Richard, I wanted to test him on his ability to control me."

"What did you do?"

"I ran away and told him if he could capture me, I was his. He gave me a head start, and I ran into the woods as a wolf."

"That must he hard chasing down a wolf."

"Yeah, it would be. But Master Richard is very good at tracking game and I didn't try to hide where I was. He found me after a couple of hours. As a werewolf, I'm not allowed to bite people, so when he caught me, it was over pretty fast. He tied my front paws together and told me to change back to human form."

"That made you his?"

"It did. He led me back to the house. My hands were still tied in front me and essentially I was his. At the house he punished me hard and put on his collar."

"I should do something like that. Make Lorhon chase me down."

"I think you should." She looked at Richard. "Master Richard, do you have any advice?"

"I know Lorhon, having met him a couple of times in a bar. If you run from him, he'll punish you. However, I think you need discipline so you understand who's in charge. So, I think Accalia's suggestion is good. When he captures you, he can put his collar on you."

Mijestic nodded. "My sisters have been mean to me. When my mother was out, they made me clean the kitchen floor while they sat around. Selena said I wasn't doing a good enough job and used a wooden spoon on me. Even Gwen has threatened to spank me. I don't why they're acting like that."

Accalia answered, "Maybe it's their way of saying they'll miss you."

Richard smiled, "Their one last chance to show you they're above you. You don't have to let them, but you like to be dominated."

"I think you're right. Have you picked out a date yet?"

Accalia answered. "Yes, the first Saturday of next month. It'll be a midnight ceremony, of course, and some members of the other packs will be there."

"I'm looking forward to it." Mijestic understood the werewolf weddings could be pretty wild as they reacted to the full moon. She wondered how Richard would handle the alpha males, as it was a tradition that the groom had to prove he was tough enough to have a female. "May I go now, Master Richard? I want to visit Lorhon."

He shook his head. "No, not yet. I need you to do something first."

That 'something' involved massaging cream on Accalia, front and back, as she stood. Under Richard's direction, most of her efforts were spent on her breasts and between her legs. Accalia was moaning by the time she was allowed to stop.

"Okay, you may go."

"Thank you, Master Richard."

Mijestic left for Lorhon after giving Accalia a kiss good bye. She flew across town to where Lorhon lived and knocked on his front door.

After a brief pause, she entered, finding him in the living room.

As she drank the wine he offered her, she told him of her day and how everyone was ordering her around and punishing her.

"I don't think you're really complaining though."

"I'm not. Just a little surprised by it. Have you found a ring for me yet?" She spoke softly.

"I'm having one made. It'll be ready soon."

"I was talking to Accalia about the collar. She suggests that I get you to chase and capture me before making me wear it. I like that idea of being chased."

He smiled. "We can do that."

"Good, that's what I want. Would you be willing to meet Accalia and Richard? They're my best friends and I want you to meet and like them too."

"Sure, as long as you understand that when I'm around, I'm your only master."

"I do."

"Good, now why don't we get you naked and go upstairs to bed before you have to leave?"

Mijestic pulled off her top. "Okay." She smiled. "That's the real reason I came over."

"Did you have a pleasant afternoon, Mijestic?" Lucinda inquired as she prepared to sit at the table.

Mijestic grinned. "Oh, yes. I had a good visit with Accalia. We talked about a few things and then I popped over to Lorhon's."

Gwendolyn whispered, "What else went pop?" as she sat next to Mijestic.

Selena passed a bowl of carrots over to Mijestic. "Glad you had a great day. Perhaps we can repeat it tomorrow."

Mijestic nodded. "Every day is new and different."

Lucinda followed the exchange and frowned. "Would you girls please stop talking in riddles? I don't like secrets kept from me, and there've been too many secrets kept from me these past weeks."

Mijestic focused her attention on her plate, hoping she wouldn't be left alone with Selena for a few days.

Accalia gave Mijestic a hug.

"I'm glad you came over. I'm so nervous." Accalia stood barefoot, wearing a short yellow flared skirt and a black t-shirt. She was also wearing thick leather cuffs on her wrists and ankles.

"Your big day is tomorrow. Is Richard nervous too?"

"He doesn't show it. He's working in the tool shed, making some new restraints for me. As if he doesn't have enough ways already to keep me under control."

"So am I going to be the only non-werewolf guest there?"

"Yeah, I hope you won't feel uncomfortable, but I really want you there."

"I'll be there. A naked witch among naked werewolves. That might be interesting."

"Don't worry. A werewolf won't force himself on you, although they need little encouragement."

Mijestic sat in the armchair and took the offered glass of wine. "I'm sure I'll be fine." She looked at the leash dangling from Accalia's collar and grabbed the end. "You wear the leash a lot lately with your collar."

"Well since I got engaged, I enjoy wearing the leash. It reminds me Richard is taking care of me."

Mijestic smiled. She knew werewolves were very social creatures and need the feeling of belonging. The leash, she reasoned, must have made Accalia more attuned to Richard being in control. "It suits you. Is Richard still disciplining you as much?"

"More, actually. He says he needs to remove my defiance."

Mijestic gave a small tug on the leash. "I suppose he figures you have a stubborn streak that needs to be addressed."

Accalia took a half step closer to Mijestic. "I guess I have that problem."

Mijestic took a sip of her wine and pulled on the leash again. "You do."

Accalia had to lower her head as she stood by the armchair. She looked at Mijestic as she placed the wine glass on the floor. The leash continued its pull on the collar and Accalia lowered herself across Mijestic's lap.

Mijestic wasn't certain why the thought of spanking Accalia intrigued her, but with the leash hanging from her submissive friend's collar, she wanted to try being the one in control for a change.

She gave Accalia's bottom a couple of smacks and folded the skirt up to expose the cheeks. She touched the soft skin with her fingertips, licked her lips, and smacked each side several times. Accalia kicked her feet and let out a small moan. Mijestic pulled down the thong to Accalia's knees. "Okay, now for the real fun to start."

Mijestic raised her hand and brought it down hard. That made a satisfying sound, and she pushed Accalia's t-shirt up, exposing her back and revealing the lack of a bra. She began to spank in earnest, watching her ass shake after each hit. As she spanked, she realized several things. One, it was rather arousing giving Accalia a spanking, with the moaning sounds she was making. Two, she liked being in control over her friend, and three, her hand hurt. She wondered if Richard and Lorhon hurt their hands during a spanking, but now knew why her mother used a hairbrush.

She took a deep breath and looked at the red cheeks. "Nice colour."

Accalia twisted her head to look back. "Yeah, they look red."

"That was fun, but my hand hurts now."

Accalia smiled. "Next time I'll get you a paddle." She rolled off Mijestic's lap and pulled her top down. "Can I pull up my panties?"

"No, leave them off. I thought we should go out for one more drink tonight, your last night as a free woman."

"I'll ask Richard." Accalia carried her panties and tossed them toward the bedroom as she made her way to the backyard.

A few minutes later Richard came into the house. "You want to take Accalia out tonight?"

"Yes, one last time before she gets married."

Richard frowned. "Okay, but stay out of trouble this one time. We don't need any problems before the wedding. If you screw up..." He pointed a finger at Mijestic, "...I will blister your butt."

Mijestic grinned. "As tempting as that sounds, I'll keep her out of trouble."

The Elephant and Rook was crowded, noisy, and filled with single men. Several gentlemen offered to join them, but Mijestic refused, along with their offers to buy drinks, remembering the trouble it caused in the past. She kept Accalia's leash in her hand when they danced, or hooked to her chair when they sat, enforcing the fact she was in control. It seemed to Mijestic, Accalia was more than content to allow her dictate what they did.

"You said Richard is making you more compliant. I guess that involves a lot more punishment."

"It does. He has an interest in using the cane on me lately. He also ordered me to wear cuffs and go without a bra this past week, and every morning he has spanked me after breakfast as a reminder he's in charge. I can't get dressed until the dishes are done either. I don't know if that'll continue after we get married, but I've stopped being defiant on anything lately."

Mijestic took a shot of whisky and a drink of beer. "It probably is doing you some good. You do look happy."

"I am. I'm getting married to the man I love. He will take good care of me. I also have the best friend in the world with me tonight. Thanks for coming over."

"I hope Richard didn't mind me taking you out tonight."

"No, not at all. He likes it when you take charge of me. I told him you spanked me and he was pleased with that."

"You told him I spanked you?"

"Yeah, well he heard the smacks you gave. By the way, he said you can discipline me any time you want." Accalia gave a hesitate smile.

Mijestic giggled. "Oh, he doesn't know how nasty I can be."

Mijestic had trouble steering her broom in a straight line, in fact discovering buildings were not something brooms were meant to collide with. She made it to Richard's home and with a little encouragement from Accalia, stayed the night. In the bedroom they quietly undressed.

Mijestic was going to wear her thong, but Accalia whispered, "Take it off. I'm naked, and so is Richard. You get naked too."

She nodded and Accalia insisted Mijestic sleep in the middle of the bed. She rested on her back with Accalia curled next to her, a hand on her chest. She listened to the quiet breathing of Accalia and the deeper sounds of Richard. She slid her hand along his side, feeling the heat from his skin. She reached his hip and gradually lifted her hand over his stomach, and touched his member with her fingertips, finding it erect and hot.

I will have trouble sleeping tonight with these thoughts running in my head.

Morning came and Mijestic was disturbed as Richard climbed out of bed.

"Hey."

He turned to smile at her. "Good morning."

"Yeah." She noticed he still had an erection. "You have a nice body."

"Thanks." He struggled to pull on his jeans, looking uncomfortable where her eyes were focused. "Breakfast in an hour."

"Okay." She sat up, letting the sheet fall from her top. "Are you going to make me stay naked like Accalia until we do the dishes?"

"Yes."

After he left the bedroom, Mijestic slid back down under the covers. Accalia changed her position, sliding a leg over her own as she slept on her stomach.

I need Lorhon. Her hand reached between her legs. Now.

Mijestic entered the kitchen with Accalia. She was naked, hungry and aroused. The sight of Richard and what he had under his jeans didn't help her thoughts any.

Breakfast was good, and as she ate, was aware of Richard glancing at her breasts. That seemed to cause her nipples to want to stand out, which increased his discrete observations, and seemed to cause an additional reaction to the nipples.

When breakfast was done, she helped Accalia to wash the dishes.

"I better get going. I'll see you later at the wedding ceremony." Mijestic went to the bedroom and sorted out her clothes. After she dressed, she proceeded to living room and wished Richard congratulations.

"Thanks. It should be interesting."

"I'm sure it'll be great. I hope you don't mind my sleeping in your bed last night."

"No, not at all. You're always welcome here. But next time you start touching me, don't stop."

Mijestic blushed. "I thought you were asleep."

"Half asleep. That's okay."

Mijestic gave Richard and Accalia a hug and headed home.

Her mother gave her a stern look when she entered the living room. "You look like you were partying all night long."

"I took Accalia out. It was her last night before getting married."

Lucinda softened her expression. "I suppose that's all right. I was wondering if you disobeyed me and went over to Lorhon's."

"No, Mother, I wouldn't disobey your order." The mention of his name made her heart beat faster.

"Good. The garden needs weeding, and you have to study your spells."

Mijestic sighed and went to her room to change. She thought of Lorhon and how she needed him. Specifically, touching Richard's member reminding her of how she wanted him. If she had known Richard was awake, she would've been very tempted to take advantage of that.

She put on a short skirt and a cropped top, deciding she might as well get a suntan while working. Mijestic carried the hoe barefoot to the garden, not wanting to wear one of her high-heeled shoes to do gardening. *One of these days I might have to get a pair of flat shoes. Ugh.*

Two hours later Mijestic finished the weeding and thinking of the hot bath she would enjoy. Gwendolyn followed her when she entered the house.

"Hey, have you heard anything about Lady Jacquelyn?"

"No, why?"

Mijestic used a spell to fill the bathtub full of hot, soapy water. It was one of the few spells Lucinda allowed in the house, telling their daughters there was little reason to suffer to keep clean.

"The wood nymphs told me she has been looking for someone to do some spells for her. The illegal kind. She is some upset with you since your last appearance at the courtyard when you outdrew her."

Mijestic undressed and tested the water with her hand. "I wish she would let that go. I'm not planning on a return there, so she can have the courtyard all to herself. If she wants to be humiliated in pubic, it's all hers."

"Okay, but I'm worried she'll do something nasty. She's a real bitch."

Mijestic lowered herself into the water. "Thanks, Gwen. I'll be careful, but a spell can always be reversed."

"Okay, enjoy your bath." She closed the bathroom door.

Mijestic closed her eyes, enjoying the warmth. Suddenly cold water seeped down to her chest. She opened her eyes to a block of ice floating in the water.

"Gwen! That's not funny." Her sister laughed as Majestic used a spell to remove the ice.

FOURTEEN

Mijestic landed a discrete distance from where the wedding ceremony was to take place. The small clearing in the forest was deep enough that the town couldn't be seen, which also meant people of the town couldn't see them. She parked her broom against a tree and took off her dress. She hadn't bothered wearing anything underneath, as she would be naked during the service. Lucinda allowed her to leave the house that way, agreeing there was little point in wearing much more than the dress.

She made her way to where a fire lighted up the evening sky, and she heard the howls and yelps of the werewolves. The service would not be long as werewolves were not known for patience. Mijestic made her way to the front of the gathering where Accalia, Richard and other members of the wedding party stood near an altar made of several sticks joined to form a pyramid shape. She greeted Accalia and Richard, then said hello to the others. They gave her a suspicious look, not sure of the presence of a non-werewolf, but they knew of her friendship with Accalia.

The service was called to order by the oldest werewolf, who would conduct the ceremony. Mijestic stood with the other women to the left of the altar. While the forest hid them from accidental observance from the townspeople, there weren't any other precautions taken to make sure they were alone. Other than Richard, Mijestic was the only non-werewolf in attendance. She was second to the alpha female of the four bridesmaids and was nervous of what would happen after the service. The male werewolves were known to be very aggressive, and it was normal for rutting to celebrate the union of two werewolves, although in this case a human and a werewolf.

The males looked powerful, and the moonlight showed off their hairy, muscular bodies. Mijestic didn't have the sense of smell were-wolves did, but her loins reacted to the pheromones and testosterone floating in the air like a fog. She saw the men had swollen penises, although not yet an erection. Behind her, where other invited were-wolves watched, the air was filled with growls and howls as they became anxious for the wedding to begin. She studied Richard. His body was nearly hairless, but his muscles were equal to that of the werewolves, save for the alpha male. The alpha male was a powerfully built man with thick limbs. Richard was not as heavily built, but he stood a head taller.

The oldest male of the pack, Varulv, stood between Accalia and Richard, and clapped his hands together once. The thirty plus werewolf guests surrounding the altar became quiet.

"The pack must grow or die. It is through the union of our members we extend the life and well-being of the pack. The union of two members is a serious matter, for we can only have one life mate, and as such the union must be taken seriously. While we encourage the bonding of our members, they must also prove themselves worthy to be allowed to be together. Thus we must test their strength. The pack, to grow strong, needs strong members."

Varulv, with coarse brown and grey hair, turned to Richard. "Are you able to prove yourself worthy of taking a female of this pack?"

"Yes, I am." Richard replied. He looked from the older werewolf to Accalia.

"Then will you accept a challenge from the alpha male of our pack?"

"Yes."

Mijestic watched as Richard and the alpha male moved to an open area. They faced each other in the centre of the on looking crowd of werewolves and locked hands as they began to wrestle. It was interesting for Mijestic to watch the two nude males battle for position. Occasionally one of them would give the other a short punch which would increase the vigour of the fight. They tumbled to ground several times, got up and wrestled again. When one fell, the other allowed him to get up again. She understood they weren't trying to hurt or win the battle, but to show the rest of the pack Richard was a credible opponent and could take care of Accalia. Long ago, the battles were much more bloody and fearsome, but the werewolves had changed the tradition in the wake of too many broken noses. The circle of werewolves gave encouragement to each fighter, and after a period of time the alpha male declared Richard was worthy of taking a mate in the pack. They shook hands and Richard joined Accalia at the altar.

The werewolves all gave cheers, and a few howled their approval. Mijestic clapped her hands and grinned at Accalia. She listened to the final words and soon Richard and Accalia were exchanging kisses. Traditionally, the couple were to change into wolves and run off together. However, with Richard only having a human form to use, they walked away together instead. The other tradition was for all the werewolves to change into wolves and, as Accalia put it, get their tails up. That meant some half-hearted fights and full hearted mating. Originally, only the alpha male and alpha female could mate. As that wasn't too popular with the rest of the werewolves, it was eventually changed so that all werewolves could mate, with the approval of the alpha male. On weddings, it was conceded that rutting was free for all.

Mijestic watched as the wolves ran around in circles, fought and licked each other. A few changed back into human form for a period, as it made fondling of the opposite sex easier.

A young blond werewolf came up to her. His erection bobbing as he walked.

"Hello, my name Terrance. You're the only human here." He smiled as his gaze wander over her body.

"Actually, I'm a witch. Mijestic."

He touched her arm. "That's all right too. I don't want you to be left out of our celebration."

"Thanks, but I don't feel left out."

He put his hands behind her back and drew her closer. "We could celebrate together."

Mijestic parted her lips as she took in a deep breath. She slipped her hands behind his neck. "Now just how would we celebrate?"

His hands dropped to her ass, and he pressed her against him.

Mijestic tilted her head back as his hard member pressed on her stomach. He kissed her throat while he shifted his hips, causing his erection to slide back and forth on her skin.

She moaned as he kissed her ears, face and then was on her mouth, pressing his tongue over hers. Her hand reached between them, rubbing his wet head with her fingers, and then she dropped to her knees, taking him in her mouth. He groaned.

"I think you're ready to go." *Young guys are always too anxious.*

"Yes, I think you're right." He dropped to his knees and turned her around, placing her on her hands and knees. He slipped his cock between her legs as she reached back to insert it in her wet vagina.

Mijestic considered it wasn't surprising he wanted to do it in that position. It wasn't her favourite way to have sex the first time, but wolves will be wolves. He did get good penetration and fondled her breasts, and all things considered, it was good sex. But it was over quicker than she wanted.

He rolled on his back and grinned at her.

She took his limp penis in her hand. "Don't look so happy or relaxed. We've just started."

Mijestic began to work on him, giving his body kisses while caressing his testicles and cock. When his erection began to form again, she put in her mouth and worked her tongue on it. It became hard and she let it slip out past her lips. She rolled on her back.

"Start sucking, big boy. My boobs need some attention."

He was eager to work on her breasts, and Mijestic was content to let him get his fill of them, then she pushed his head down.

He took the hint and Mijestic sighed as he played with her pussy.

Mijestic considered the second time was much better than the first. She also decided she better depart, despite his protests, before the other werewolves decided she was an interesting outsider. She didn't want to get into another orgy, trying to limit those to just a few times in a year.

She hurried back to where she parked her broom and hung up her dress on a tree limb. She could still hear the howls coming from where the ceremony was held and sighed. *They sure can to party. I wonder what Lorhon and Mother would say to a naked service?* She grinned at the thought of even asking them.

Mijestic found her broom, but not her dress. Puzzled, she looked around and entered the forest, thinking the wind blew it somewhere.

She heard a whisper and took another step inside the forest. The whisper grew louder and the sound of a giggle came from a nearby tree. She approached the oak tree, peering into the shadows. Another stifled giggle.

"Hello?" She looked around, feeling very naked and vulnerable in the thick forest. "Do you have my dress?"

"Maybe," came the whispered reply. The sound of muffled giggles came shortly after.

"Eurydice? Echo? Is that you?" Mijestic was familiar with the wood nymphs that were friends with Gwendolyn.

"Hi, Mijestic." The voices were light with a hint of laughter.

"Can I have my dress back please?" She stood with her hands on her hips.

After a moment of waiting Mijestic stepped around the oak tree. She saw nothing past the nearby trees and leaned back on the oak tree. "Come on, I need my dress back. This isn't funny." She knew wood nymphs could be mischievous and like to play games. They were also amorous and enjoyed both male and female bodies.

Suddenly a warm hand touched her arm, pulling it to the tree trunk. Another hand pulled her waist, holding her. Mijestic looked down, seeing slender female arms slide out of the oak tree to hold her gently against the tree trunk.

Wood Nymphs adopted trees to live in and it seemed she had come into an area they inhabited.

"Come on girls. I don't have time to play with you. Can I have my dress back please?"

More giggles. "Soon."

Mijestic signed. She didn't resist against the hands that reached out and held her. The nymphs slowly appeared. The slim, beautiful creatures cautiously approached her, giggling as they touched her. They were dressed in forest clothing, green leaves and thin strips of cloth.

Mijestic stood frozen as the shy creatures pressed against her.

Fingertips grazed across her skin. Delicate but insistent, soft light scratches on her warm skin. An occasional hot breath grazed across her neck.

She moaned, which only made them more insistent. She felt touches everywhere. Whispers and light laughter. The smell of crushed leaves and wood penetrated her senses. It was hard to push back at the many touches. It was difficult to see the nymphs in the low light, and sometimes they looked like a bush or a thin tree, other times like a beautiful woman.

There was slow but insistent tugs on her arms and legs, gradually pulling Mijestic down to the forest floor. She resisted, but relented to their constant pull. She considered her options. She could give in to the rather pleasant touches, or she could fight back against the wood nymphs. Fighting back consisted of two options, one was physically trying to break free. She was certainly outnumbered, but the wood nymphs were not violent and likely would react to her struggle to get free by running away. She, being a witch, could also use a spell to free herself. But there was a problem with both methods to get her freedom.

One was that while she would be free, she would still be without her dress. The other problem would be that the wood nymphs would tell Gwendolyn what she did. Her sister would be upset with her and if she told her mother that Mijestic was rude to friends, out would come the hairbrush.

Mijestic decided to make only a token resistance to the wood nymphs, hoping she would get her dress back at the end of the night. She had to admit the wood nymphs were experienced in how to touch. Gentle, but with a degree of forcefulness, fingers traced across her skin.

She wasn't sure how many wood nymphs there were. They had a tendency to appear and then disappear into the surrounding trees. But there were at least four and perhaps half-a-dozen. Her limbs were lightly restrained. She could move them to a degree, but any attempt to push away met with a firm resistance. Her legs were parted, and she decided she might as well accept she had lost control of the situation.

Touches continued, lips and tongues brushed her skin. Her nipples were both sucked on at the same time. A breast was firmly pressed to her mouth, and she was obligated to open her lips and take a mouthful of the intrusion. Warmth filled her groin and tender touches between her legs excited her. She moaned. She groaned. She gasped. She wanted to them to finish her now, but the wood nymphs weren't in any hurry.

They giggled. They chatted in whispers. They took their time in pleasing her, teasing her to higher and higher levels of ecstasy.

Mijestic tightened her muscles. Her back arched, and a pleasure vibrated along her being. She lay panting on the forest floor, too weak to move.

Time passed, and Mijestic sat up. She looked around and at first saw only tress and green foliage. Then she made out Eurydice and Echo in their leaf dresses, combining nudity and coverage in green leaves.

"Hey, thanks for the intervention. But I still need my dress back."

They snickered. "You look so delicious naked."

Mijestic could hardly argue with that. "Thanks. You and Eurydice are sexy too."

Echo smiled and held up her dress in her fingertips by her shoulder. "Here's your dress. You should come and play with us more often. Gwen will tell you we're fun to play with."

"I'm sure." Mijestic took her dress and quickly put it on. "I hope you don't mind I really have to fly."

"Sure, that's okay. I hope we can see you again soon."

Mijestic hurried to her broom and took off, not wanting to find out if the wood nymphs decided on another round of pleasing the witch,

She parked her broom by the door and stumbled to her bedroom. She dragged off her dress and fell asleep, dreaming of dancing trees that chased her.

FIFTEEN

Lorhon arrived at the Witches' Guild lodge and walked up to the entrance where Mijestic waited with Lucinda.

Mijestic gave him a hug and kiss as Lucinda watched and crossed her arms.

"If you two have finished saying hello, we should go in."

Their footsteps sounded hollow on the wood floor that was normally filled with witches during meetings. They made their way to the offices at the back of the lodge, behind doors marked 'Employees Only'. The president stood as they entered her spacious office, frowning at Lorhon.

After they sat on the three chairs facing the hand carved desk, Helga spoke. "We don't normally allow anyone but witches in our lodge and a warlock is pushing the limits of our tolerance." She glared at Lorhon.

Lorhon smiled as he replied. "Thank you for your indulgence."

"You seem to believe you have something to say that will change our policies regarding one of our member's association with a warlock. I can't imagine what that would be, but speak up." She crossed her arms.

Lorhon nodded. "It must be difficult being the president. You must spend much time doing work for the Guild with little time for your own personal needs."

"That's a sacrifice I'm willing to make."

"I understand. The warlocks' Guild president has the same problem, trying to find time for social desires. I'm a good friend of his, as a matter of fact. His name is Oberon, and he's mentioned your name in passing. Perhaps you've met him?"

Helga's jaw dropped and her complexion lightened.

Lorhon smiled. "I thought that allowing witches and warlocks to have a relationship would be beneficial for both Guilds. We could learn from each other and present a stronger voice to the town council and mayor."

"A very good point, Lorhon. I agree completely and will make sure the Witches' Guild won't object to your union with Mijestic." She spoke rapidly and stood. "Thank you for coming and have a good day."

As they walked back to the exit, Mijestic whispered, "What happened there? Did Lorhon put an agreement spell on her?"

Lucinda frowned. "There wasn't any need for a spell. As Lorhon knew, and I just found out, our president is having an affair with the president of the Warlocks' Guild." She spoke to Lorhon. "You're a horrible man for not telling us that sooner. I hate secrets."

Mijestic smiled as she sat at the dinner table next to Lorhon. Lucinda had invited Lorhon, with some hesitation, to have dinner with the family. With equal hesitation, Lorhon agreed.

Selena passed a plate of potatoes to him. "Try them, I made them myself. I assure you I didn't put a spell on them." She smiled sweetly.

Mijestic retorted. "Don't mind her. The potatoes are fine. Mother doesn't allow magic in the house."

Lorhon took the plate. "I'm sure they're fine." He took only a small portion of the potatoes.

Mijestic frowned. "Selena, why can't you be nice? We're getting married and I want you to get along with him."

"I'm still emotionally scarred from how he treated me."

Gwendolyn smirked, "Right, that's a stretch to blame him for jumping in the sack with a different woman every week."

Lucinda tapped the table with her finger. "That's enough bickering. We've a guest here and he shouldn't have to listen to our problems."

Lorhon picked up his fork. "Are these potatoes really okay to eat?"

Lucinda announced in a clear voice. "All the food here is safe to eat. I can assure you if there are any problems with anything on this table, the consequences for those preparing the meal would be severe." She looked at Selena. "Am I clear about this?"

Selena nodded.

Mijestic filled her own plate and noticed Selena's jaws working as she mouthed silent words. *That witch did put a spell on the food and is now removing it. If Mother sees that the hairbrush will have quite a workout later.*

Mijestic was glad when the meal was finished, even though it meant Lorhon would head home soon. It seemed the potatoes were all right after all, at least during the evening he didn't show any ill effects.

After dinner they adjourned to the living room. Mijestic was surprised when he sat on the couch between Selena and Gwendolyn. He put his arm around Selena and Mijestic saw the suspicious look she gave him.

Lorhon spoke loud enough for everyone in the room, "I'm sorry for causing you any distress in the past. I treated you poorly and ask for forgiveness. I was careless about your feelings."

Selena gave out a heavy sigh. "You're forgiven. I guess I can't hold a grudge if you will be my brother-in-law. But if you ever screw around with her heart, jump on your broom and don't stop flying until you reach the moon. Because that'll be the only safe place if I come looking for you."

"Fair enough." He smiled and gave her a hug.

"What about me?" Gwendolyn asked. "Don't I get a heartfelt apology too?"

He grinned. "Na. That was a just a good, practical joke. It lasted a little long, but still funny."

Gwendolyn punched him on the shoulder. "I'm not laughing." She crossed her arms and pouted.

Mijestic looked her sister. "Gwen, the spell was taken off and you're still not wearing a bra. So how do you figure he needs to apologize for that spell if that's how you like to dress?"

"It's the principle of the thing."

"All right, I'm sorry for leaving the spell on too long." He chuckled.

"That's better, but not very sincere."

Lorhon stood. "I better be going. Thank you for your hospitality."

She gave Lorhon a long kiss, and he departed, roaring off in his broom.

Selena even gave him a wave goodbye, showing her anger was over. Mijestic was certain Gwendolyn was past her resentment and it seemed her mother was no longer harbouring ill feelings about him. That left the ring as the next stage, and she hoped he would bring it to her soon so she could live with him.

Mijestic headed off to bed, realizing it had been a long time since she had slept in her own bed so many nights in a row. *Almost like when I was just a teenager. Maybe I was a little too wild as mother suggested, although 'prowling around like a tomcat', was harsh.*

She undressed and climbed into bed when she heard a noise outside her bedroom window. Hoping that it was Lorhon who wanted to sneak back into her room, she flung open the window and the shutters. She looked into the darkness lit by the full moon and saw a wolf.

"Accalia!"

The wolf bounded into her bedroom and stood up on her hind legs as Mijestic gave her a hug. A few minutes later Accalia changed into her human form.

"I wanted to hear how it went at the Witches' Guild."

Mijestic related the story. "So everything is good now, except Mother won't allow me to go out at night."

"So, no sex?"

She shook her head. "Just hot thoughts about what he will do to me later."

"Well, you're naked. I'm naked." She took Mijestic's hand. "Once you get married, we may not get another chance."

Mijestic leaned forward and gave her a kiss. "Let's make it a night to remember."

She put her arms around Accalia and kissed her lips as they stood next to the bed. She kissed repeatedly, lingering longer each time. Accalia started to pull on Mijestic's neck, trying to hold her as she opened her mouth. Mijestic reached back and gave her ass a smack.

"No, I'm in control of you. Understand?"

Accalia loosened her grip. "Yes, I understand." Her words came out in a hot rush.

"Good." She manoeuvred Accalia close to bed, kissing her as one hand played with an engorged nipple. She heard a low moan from Accalia as she tilted her head back. Mijestic took advantage of her exposed throat, caressing the flesh with her lips as Accalia began to go limp in her arms.

She pushed Accalia on the bed, placing her legs between Accalia's. Firmly she took Accalia's hands and placed them above her head, pinning them there with one of her own as the other hand worked on a breast. Mijestic kissed Accalia, pushing her tongue past the open lips.

As the kiss continued, Mijestic's hand released her wrists and traced down her arm, dragging her nails along the skin. She relinquished her grip on Accalia's breast and slid her hands down to her rear.

Accalia gasped as Mijestic seized each cheek in her hands and kneaded the flesh. Her back arched, and she kept her hands crossed above her head.

Mijestic dropped her head on Accalia's breasts and began to lay a carpet of kisses on them. Accalia moaned as Mijestic moved her hands up to squeeze her breasts, sucking on each nipple. Mijestic pressed a thigh between Accalia's legs. The contact felt warm and wet, and Accalia let out a series of moans. Mijestic lowered her breasts on Accalia's mouth, and the werewolf placed one hand on top of Mijestic's head, eagerly licking and kissing the flesh.

For a short time Mijestic allowed Accalia to work on her breasts as she rolled her thigh back and forth between her legs. Then she pulled away, moving down as she touched Accalia's hot skin with her fingertips. Mijestic pushed apart Accalia's knees and licked between her legs. Accalia raised her hips to press Mijestic's tongue harder against her and began to rock her hips back and forth as Mijestic pressed a finger into the wet slit. Mijestic added another finger inside, listening to the groans becoming louder and deeper. A primeval growl came out and for a moment fur began to appear on Accalia's skin.

Mijestic smiled, remembering Accalia telling her that occasionally when she had an orgasm, she could lose control of her body momentarily. She looked at Accalia; closed eyes, arms above her head and back arched. Accalia gasped one last time and dropped her hips onto the mattress. Slowly Mijestic slid up alongside of Accalia, brushing the damp hair from her face.

"Maybe I can do you now." Accalia puffed out.

"Just relax, my werewolf friend. All is good." She gave her a kiss. "I did what I did because I care about you, not because I wanted a favour in return."

"Hmm." Accalia turned on her side, wiggled downward until her head was at Mijestic's chest.

Mijestic stroked her hair as the hot breath on her breasts become slower and deeper. Shortly later a few twitches of Accalia's limbs showed she was asleep and Mijestic closed her eyes, dreaming of running through a forest with Accalia.

Dawn hadn't quite arrived yet, but Mijestic woke to the soft glow in the room from the full moon. She was now sleeping on the other side of the bed but the werewolf's face was still buried between her breasts. Her nipples felt full and sore as Accalia began to stir.

"Good morning."

Accalia mumbled something.

"I think you have to go before it gets light outside." She knew of the usual rules Richard had for her. A warm tongue traced the outline of her nipple and Mijestic moaned. "Were you doing that all night?"

"I think I did. Mostly during my sleep." Accalia looked up at Mijestic. "I woke up a couple of times with my hand between your legs too. I stopped because I didn't want to wake you."

"That would have been okay to have my sleep interrupted that way." She smiled. "Now you better get your tail moving."

"I guess you're right. Thank you for last night. That was really special to me."

Mijestic smiled. "It was special to me too. Next time I might tie you up to my bed and really do things to you."

Accalia grinned. "I'll bring the rope." She dropped to the floor and began to transform into a wolf.

Mijestic watched as the wolf circled the room once, looked at her, and jumped out of the window.

After Accalia left, Mijestic yawned as she made her way into the kitchen, searching for a cup of tea.

Selena handed her a cup, asking "Who was the late night visitor? I heard your bed squeak and a lot of moans."

Mijestic blushed. "Sorry. Accalia came to see me."

"Really? You and the werewolf? I thought you two were just friends."

"Our first time. For that anyway."

"I'm surprised you haven't hooked up before. You can tell she adores you every time she's over here."

"I care for her too. Thanks for the tea." Mijestic turned to leave, not wanting to continue the conversation on her relationship with Accalia.

"Wait, I didn't mean to embarrass you. I will miss having you around."

"I'll miss you too. But I'll be back lots to visit." Mijestic returned to the kitchen and leaned against the doorframe.

"I hope so. If not, I'll visit you. What are your plans for today?"

"Accalia and Richard are coming over to visit Lorhon and me at his place."

"Hmm. Richard and Lorhon in the same room? Two very dominant males and I suspect you will obey to either of them if they gave you an order. That could be interesting."

"Richard won't do that to me." *I hope.*

"You're right. He's a good man. But, if you ever need to talk to someone, remember I'm still your big sister who'll look after you."

Mijestic thought that now she was moving out, she was getting along with Selena. *Better late than never I suppose.*

Mijestic had trouble sitting still, continually getting up and looking out the living room window. Richard and Accalia had agreed to come over to Lorhon's home for afternoon drinks, and she hoped the meeting would go well. *I'm sure Accalia will like Lorhon, but it will be interesting how Richard acts. In a way, I've two masters, and I want to please both of them.*

"Mijestic, kneel by the chair and calm down." Lorhon pointed at an armchair that faced an identical one across from a coffee table. Like the couch along the wall, they were made with dark leather.

She complied, hearing the growl in his voice. Kneeling wasn't easy wearing stilettos, but she remembered how she was taught by Richard. She spread her knees by a foot, taking care not to cause a snag in her fishnet stockings, and clasped her hands behind her back. She straightened her back, making her low cut bra press against her black sheer blouse. Her accessories included matching wrist and ankle cuffs. The cuffs were wide, made of a dull white metal and locked. She declined to put on the collar, deciding a ring had to be on her finger first. Mijestic saw Lorhon look at her with mild surprise at her kneeling position and nodded his approval.

If you're wondering where I learned that, I think you'll figure that out when Richard and Accalia come over.

Mijestic found she was calming down, although she wasn't certain if the kneeling position was doing it or because of the commanding voice of Lorhon.

She heard the door knocker and her heart jumped. She watched as Lorhon casually walked to the door, opened it and ushered in Richard and Accalia. Mijestic saw Richard had put on a dress shirt, pleased he had taken the effort to dress up. Accalia wore a short red skirt open on both sides to the hip. As usual, she had bare legs. Stockings could be an annoyance for a werewolf wanting to change states in a hurry. Her pale yellow blouse showed the faint outline of nipple clips. Accalia wore red leather cuffs and a collar with a leather leash attached. A chain went from a ring in her collar to inside her blouse and, Mijestic assumed, to the nipple clips. She was also barefoot as Richard led her into the home.

Richard held polished oak wood pieces under his arm and he gave Mijestic a wink as he turned to speak to Lorhon. "Thank you for the invitation to visit you. I made a gift for you to share with Mijestic." He presented the wood pieces to Lorhon, plus several small padlocks.

Mijestic looked on with interest. One piece was easy to identify, a long hinged board with two holes at opposite ends. She decided it could be used to hold wrists, or more likely, ankles, for the other piece was a triangle with one large hole and two smaller ones. Each of the holes were hinged and lockable, to be used to restrain a head and hands. *Interesting he brought that over. I'll bet Accalia told him I won't wear his collar until I've an engagement ring, and this is a substitute for a collar and cuffs.*

Mijestic remained kneeling as Richard and Lorhon sat in the armchairs. Accalia knelt next to Richard's chair and gave Mijestic a smile.

Now that's a proper sub look. Bare legs, see-through top, collar and cuffs. Probably isn't wearing any panties under that split skirt. She looks so submissive with that leash. I hope Richard and Lorhon decide to take advantage of us, perhaps with a bit of punishment.

Mijestic served wine and nibbles and returned to her kneeling position next to Lorhon. Her wish for punishment came true, but not the way she expected.

Richard and Lorhon talked about the town politics, agreeing the mayor had been in power too long but there was little opposition to her rule. They agreed the Justiciar was an old pervert, but didn't mind his rulings. They discussed the various council members and their position of power. For Mijestic, the conversation was torture. She held her tongue, although she wanted to add her comments on how unfair the Justiciar was in handing out sentences, although on reflection, being stripped nude in public was exciting. Still, she wondered how the men could talk about politics when they had two women willing to be put in restraints. *They need to re-evaluate their priorities. Just when you figure men only think about sex, they do something really strange. They talk.*

Richard chuckled. "The big problem with the Justiciar and his sentences is that prosecutor loves to have women punished. Any woman that comes in front of the Justiciar, she pushes for them to be stripped naked and paddled. That prosecutor has a nasty streak towards women, and the Justiciar goes along with her suggestions. I suspect they see each other outside of working hours."

Lorhon agreed. "They have a cosy arrangement. That's not the only secret at town hall. Our mayor, a wizard, certainly does things in mysterious ways."

"You're talking about the Nonday."

Lorhon smiled, "Yes, who knows the real reason that day was created."

Accalia looked up at Richard. "Master Richard, I thought it was to help to give us extra nights of full moons?"

"That was one reason given to create Nonday, but there are suspicions of the real reason. It's one many mysteries we have, such as the zipper paradox."

Mijestic asked, "The zipper paradox?" She quickly added, "Master Lorhon."

"The zipper paradox refers to where the zipper comes from. Do you know where the zipper for your clothes comes from?"

"The tailor uses a copying spell to make zippers."

"Correct, but where did the first zipper come from? We don't have the technology to manufacture one."

Mijestic thought for a moment. "Oh. Maybe the first zipper didn't come from Elfwind."

Lorhon nodded. "Indeed. But that begs the question, where is that someplace else besides Elfwind?"

Mijestic recalled Lorhon told her that the Great Forest had an end and showed the Forever Lake was not the only lake. And Theron said something about tequila that the plant it comes from doesn't grow here. "The truth is kept from us. Perhaps the zipper came from beyond the mountains you told me about."

"Maybe it did. Someday we may find out."

Richard stood. "Thank you for your hospitality. Perhaps we can get together again soon at our place."

"Yes, I'm looking forward to seeing some other devices you've made and perhaps how to use them."

"That can be arranged."

Mijestic listened to the conversation. *What's wrong with today?* "That sounds like fun." She smiled and gave Accalia a hug.

Accalia spoke up. "Before we leave, Master Lorhon, can we see how the new restraints look on Mijestic? I'm sure she'd love to try them on."

Lorhon nodded. "Of course." He picked up the wood triangular piece of wood. "Mijestic, please remove your top." He turned to Richard. "I believe the appearance of restraints is enhanced by the removal of clothing."

"Agreed." Richard watched Mijestic as she unbuttoned her blouse.

Mijestic took off her blouse. She felt her breasts expand and press against the bra, trying to pop out of their confines. Mijestic took a deep breath as Lorhon locked the wood collar around her neck and she raised her hands to the smaller holes. She couldn't see below the wood block and decided that gave Lorhon another advantage with the restraint.

"I like it." Lorhon stood back as he examined her.

"You may need these." Richard passed over keys. "Eventually you may need to undo the locks."

Lorhon looked at Mijestic after they left. "I believe this device will come in very handy."

"I'm sure you do. I hope you're not planning to use this on me often. I feel very helpless just standing here. Let me go now, please."

The result was exactly as Mijestic hoped. She was left in the restraint and given a hard spanking after her skirt was removed. She cried out as he walloped her ass with one hand, while using his other hand to steady her by placing it between her legs.

When he stopped, Mijestic moaned. She knew he felt her wetness and there was little point in pretending what she wanted. "I can hardly wait until I get to stay the night with you."

"It'll be soon. I believe the ring should be ready tomorrow."

Mijestic smiled. "I'm so looking forward to seeing it."

SIXTEEN

Mijestic returned home, her thoughts whirling around. The ring was foremost, but the wearing of a collar and other restraints also demanded her attention. Then there was the discipline she would receive from Lorhon that she feared and anticipated. Finally, the question of the zipper paradox bothered her. Was it possible there was another place where the first zipper came from? She found it hard to believe there was another place besides Elfwind, but the evidence was pointing in that direction.

She decided to talk to her mother, approaching her in the kitchen as she was preparing a potion. Selena was helping her measure out the exact amount of dry ingredients into a bowl.

"May I ask you something, Mother?"

"Of course, dear." Lucinda didn't turn around as she let a teaspoon of a grey powder fall into the bowl.

"Have you heard of the zipper paradox?"

"Yes, the zipper paradox refers to several items on Elfwind that can be created only through the use of a copying spell. The zipper is the most obvious, but we also have the same problem with other objects that cannot be manufactured here without the use of magic." She turned to Mijestic. "This is a discussion normally found with the senior witches. I assume Lorhon brought the subject up?"

"Yes, when Richard and Accalia were visiting. Lorhon also told me the Great Forest has an end, and he's shown me a lake besides the Forever Lake. There's a lot more to this world than Elfwind, isn't there?"

"According to the old books, there is another place besides Elfwind."

Selena joined in. "I've read one book where it claims we only exist on one of many realms, and the other realms are not aware of us. One of those realms is where the zipper originated." She shrugged. "Just a theory."

"It may be just a theory, but maybe there's something to it. And why do they teach us the Great Forest goes on forever when it doesn't?"

Lucinda sighed. "I guess I shouldn't have kept the truth from you this long. Mijestic, magic created everything in Elfwind by an ancient wizard. The wizard could do this by limiting the size of Elfwind. If you, or anyone, try to go past the boundary of the Great Forest where the mountains begin, then you'll disappear forever. Nothing exists past the mountains."

Mijestic nodded. "If that's true, then how did a zipper arrive here from another realm? I mean, didn't someone have to leave Elfwind, go to another realm where zippers are manufactured, and bring one back?"

Lucinda frowned. "That might be true, but promise me you'll never try to leave Elfwind."

"I'm not planning to. I'm happy here and in love with Lorhon. Why would I ever leave Elfwind?"

The next day Mijestic wandered through the market streets with Gwendolyn, picking out groceries. It wasn't as bad as she remembered to shop for food and having her sister's company made the trip enjoyable.

"Thanks for coming with me, Gwen."

"I was shocked when you volunteered to go to the market. You're finally being a help around the house and now you're going to move out." She gave Mijestic a hug. "I will miss you."

"I'll miss you too." Mijestic looked across at the next merchant table where turnips were being sold. The turnips didn't attract her attention, but she recognized the customer examining the vegetables. She pointed at him and whispered, "I've met him before."

Gwendolyn nodded, "Yeah, that's Vadith. He owns a shoe shop I go to."

Mijestic stared for a moment longer and turned away when he looked up and smiled at her. *A shoe store? He was the clerk in the permit office.*

"Where's his store?"

"On Cobham Street. You've seen it, High Way Shoes. They specialize in stilettos."

"I've been there, but never saw him."

"He's there occasionally. His daughters run the store most of the time."

According to Lorhon he practically owns Elfwind. So why does he work as a clerk, own a shoe shop and shop for vegetables? I've got to visit that store and talk to him. Also to get more shoes. Can't have enough of those.

Cobham Street, also known as Politician's Road, was a crooked and twisted road. High Way Shoes was near the middle of the shops and Mijestic stepped inside. Rust coloured brick gave the store a permanent appearance, with the single paned window displaying an array of shoes. She entered through the wood door that rang a bell as she entered. The smell of leather and the array of shoes with thin straps initially took away her original objective, but she soon recovered. She looked around the shop with a small area to try on the shoes. A clerk stepped around the counter and greeted her.

"Hi, can I help you?"

She smiled at the clerk, a pretty brunette with long, wavy hair. "Hi, is the owner in?"

The clerk gave a fresh red lipstick, white teeth smile. "May I ask why you want to see him?"

"He owes me something."

The brunette frowned and headed to back where the beaded curtain separated the back from the customers.

A moment later a man entered the shop, followed by the brunette.

"I'm Vadith. How can help you?"

Mijestic turned from fondling a pair of red shoes and smiled. "Hi. I have a question."

He looked at her, surprised for a moment. "Mijestic."

"You know me?"

"I do. Now what do I owe you?"

"I think you owe me some answers. You work at the permit office and you own a shoe store. You're very powerful and need not do anything, yet I saw you at the market buying produce. You seem to be everywhere."

"I like to keep myself busy."

"That's not exactly an answer. I think you're hiding something."

"Interesting. Why would you say that?" He gave a faint smile and raised his eyebrows.

"Where do you get your shoes from?"

"We make them here."

"Magic?"

"Where are you going with these questions? I don't feel a need to answer them, to be frank."

"Look, I heard about the zipper paradox, found out the Great Forest has an end, that Elfwind may have be created by magic. My woman's intuition tells me you're involved somehow, so I'm wondering if all these oddities are tied together and where you fit in."

Vadith nodded. "You are very perceptive, Mijestic. However, my advice is for you to just accept Elfwind for what it is and to concentrate on your upcoming marriage to Lorhon."

"I'm not put off that easy."

"I'm not surprised to hear that. You have a rather determined personality. That can be good to have, but also has gotten you into trouble before. I suggest you stop searching for answers that cannot be found here. Now, is there anything else I can do for you?"

"Yes, do you have these in black?" She held up the red shoe.

———

Mijestic walked home with two pairs of shoes, musing over her conversation with Vadith. *He knows more than he told me, although I guess he didn't have to talk to me at all. Interesting that he knew I was engaged to Lorhon. How did he know that?*

She went straight to her room, putting her new shoes with the other dozens of pairs in the shrinking closet. *It's a good thing Lorhon's house has bigger closets.*

Mijestic decided she better get busy on her share of the housework.

Selena, as was customary, was working in the kitchen. Mijestic noted her wardrobe had changed to shorter skirts and lighter fabric tops. Her social life had become more active as well. Although she kept to her same girlfriends, Mijestic saw a better attitude towards men and suspected she might date one again. Someday.

"How's things, Selena?"

"Good. I had too much to drink last night. I tried tequila."

"Oh, that can be dangerous. Men were around I take it."

"How do you know that?"

"Women like gin. Men, tequila. The result is the same. Did you get lucky?"

"I did okay."

"All right, I won't press for details. Have you ever met a man named Vadith?"

"Hmm, he's the mayor's partner."

"What? How come I didn't know that?"

"He keeps a low profile and the mayor never mentions him. I found out from the wood nymphs that seem to know all the gossip."

"Sex and gossip go together." Mijestic began cleaning the floor, wondering how Vadith could be a government clerk, own a shoe store and be the mayor's partner. Clearly he didn't need to work and she wondered what he was up to.

SEVENTEEN

"We need some potatoes and vegetables." Selena announced to Mijestic as she began to clean up the table after lunch. "Can you go to the market before dinner?"

Mijestic put away the plates into the cupboard. "Sure."

"If you go now, you'll get back in time so we can use them for dinner. The cupboard is a little bare right now."

Mijestic smiled. "It's a nice day for a walk to the market."

Witches typically weren't scared of being alone, partly because they were sometimes one of those creatures people were scared of. However Mijestic was apprehensive as she made her way to the market, carrying an empty, environmentally friendly bag made from pigskin. She left her broom at home, finding it made it difficult to manoeuvre around other shoppers and the running children. If a child was hit on the head with a broom, the blame usually was pointed at the broom rider.

As she made her way past the clusters of people she felt she was being followed. Witches have an ability to detect when things weren't quite right, although they were also the ones who sometimes caused the 'not quite right' problem. In this case she heeded to the feeling and changed her course to a less used street where anyone, or anything, could be seen. The street was narrow, and while straight, rose in a series of uneven mounds to a T intersection. It was also quite deserted, save for herself. That didn't bother her, although it was not the place particularly suited a woman in high heels and a short skirt. She reached the end of the quiet street and turned around, waiting for an obvious follower to reveal itself. When no one appeared, she turned around to consider whether to continue her upward journey or return to the main street.

That was the moment the demon revealed herself, stepping out into the intersection. Mijestic gave a small gasp, and although she wasn't frightened of demons, her appearance was disconcerting, made slightly ridiculous by a red hat.

The demon, like the rest of her kind, didn't have the nicest features, a slender, misshapen skull with thin hair. Their faces were commonly pockmarked with warts and oddly placed tufts of hair. Their hooked noses were large and their black eyes narrow. They were of normal height, but stood with hunched shoulders. The men were even worse looking.

Mijestic frowned at the demon. They had a reputation of being evil, but also she knew it was more complicated than that. It wasn't that they just choose to do evil. They didn't care what they did was right or wrong, good or bad, or the truth or a lie. Their goal was to collect gold, silver or the rarest of all metals, aluminium foil. They were willing to do anything to obtain those metals, such as doing illegal spells. Demons were not known for their smarts, or as witches were fond of saying, a few bristles short of a broom. However they knew magic and memorized any spells they came across.

"What do you want?" Mijestic sneered at the demon. "A cure for the ugly?"

The demon grinned with yellow, pointed teeth, looking rather hideous. She lisped a few phrases and suddenly Mijestic didn't have to worry about the demon.

Mijestic staggered for a moment, but adjusted her balance to the change of where she was standing. The sidewalk was now level and made with concrete and not uneven bricks. She stared at the buildings crowded against each other as vehicles rolled down the asphalt streets.

A few pedestrians glanced at her as they walked by. Mijestic was used to being stared at. Long legs under a short skirt had a tendency to do that, especially coupled with a tight fitting top. She assumed she was the best looking woman in town, wherever this town was.

Some people might not react well suddenly transported to a strange town, but Mijestic was confident in her ability to handle any situation. Thanks to her mother insisting she study magic spells, that there was a way to help her find her way back to Elfwind. It meant following clues and being very honest when asked a question. She said the required magic phrases and began to walk. It didn't matter where she went, or even if she stood still, a clue would appear. Standing still seemed to draw too much attention to her and she decided walking would let her observe more of the strange place where she had been deposited.

The sidewalk, with its even, flat top, impressed her. She wondered how they cut the white rock so it fitted with the next square block. The vehicles were noisy, but seemed much faster than horse and carriages. As a bonus, they didn't smell like horses either.

Mijestic crossed the street with the other pedestrians, after determining the reason for the walk lights. So far, other than a few men watching her walk, her movement in the new town was uneventful. She wanted to change that and began to follow the ninth - a number known to witches as being sacred - person she saw, a man in a black suit. He walked a short distance, crossed the street, and entered a coffee shop. She figured out it was a coffee shop, the large sign proclaiming it to have the best coffee in town.

She did not understand what coffee was, but the smell in the shop was pleasant. She looked around and noticed a boy, perhaps approaching his teens, stare at her. Mijestic had seen that look on young men before. *Check with me in another decade.* She continued to look around and spotted an empty table and claimed it. She had nothing to drink yet, but that wasn't a problem for a witch. Mijestic watched what another woman was carrying from the counter and duplicated it. A latte sat in front of her and she experimented with a small sip.

It wasn't anything like she had before, but decided she liked it. She took another sip and looked up to see the boy standing by her table. He had messy, brown hair, a T-shirt with a superhero on it and blue jeans.

"How did you do that?"

"Do what?"

"Make the cup suddenly appear."

"Magic. I used a duplicating spell."

"You can do magic?"

"Yes. I'm a witch."

He processed the information for a moment. "You can copy anything?"

"Pretty much. Small items are easy. Bigger things take a lot of energy and can hurt the balance of nature."

He pulled out a plastic figurine. "Can you copy my Superman?"

Mijestic shrugged. "Sure." She whispered a few phrases and there were two figurines.

"Wow! That's really cool. I bet you could make a lot of money doing that."

"I suppose, but I'm not after money. I need to find a way to get home."

"Where's that?"

"Elfwind."

"Never heard of it."

A teenaged girl came up to him, carrying two cups. "Michael, I told you to find us a table." She looked at Mijestic. "Sorry, he's not afraid to talk to strangers."

"That's all right. You can sit here."

The blonde girl looked around at the full café. "Thanks, I guess it's busy here." She sat with Michael at the small table.

The girl, unlike the boy, was dressed neatly in a blue top and tight jeans. "I'm Jeanette."

"Mijestic."

"She's a witch who can do magic spells."

"Michael, don't be rude."

"That's all right. I am a witch."

Michael added more information. "She's also lost."

Jeanette looked concerned. "Where do you need to go?"

"A place called Elfwind."

She shook her head. "Is that a place or a store? I know where a lot of stores are."

"A place."

"Well, my mom will meet us here after she finishes her shopping. We can ask her."

"That might help." Mijestic shifted in her chair and crossed her legs away from the visual inspection of Michael.

Jeanette looked at the legs and her shoes. "I like your shoes. Where did you get them, not that my mom would let me wear anything like that?"

"A shop called High Way Shoes."

"Oh, I know that place. They carry only shoes with a real high heel."

Mijestic's jaw dropped. "Really? Where are they located?"

Jeanette pointed down the street. "It's just two blocks that way, and then turn left. It's in the middle of the street. It's an old looking store, but has really neat shoes."

Mijestic stood. "Thanks, Jeanette, for your help."

The second High Way Shoes looked a lot like the one on Elfwind. Mijestic entered and saw one of the daughters behind the small counter.

"I need to speak with Vadith."

The woman's eyes opened wide, and hurried past the beaded curtain, calling out "Father, we have a big problem."

Mijestic crossed her arms and waited. She was determined to give a stern look when he appeared, although she wanted to look at the shoes on display.

Vadith entered. "Mijestic." He let out a long sigh. "How the devil did you end up on Earth and find our shop?"

"A demon sent me here, and I found your shop because you didn't have the imagination to think of a different name for this shoe store."

He frowned. "The name, and the store, has to be the same on both realms, otherwise the gateway would crumble." He beckoned with his finger. "Follow me."

Mijestic followed him through the curtain, down past the narrow hallway jammed with shoe boxes, and through another beaded curtain.

"Welcome back to Elfwind."

Mijestic looked at the shoe store. "It's good to be back." She turned to face him. "So, I guess this solves the zipper paradox. How did you make this gateway?"

"I'm a Grand Wizard. I created Elfwind a few hundred years ago."

"You did everything? Including Nonday?"

"Nonday helps keep Elfwind and Earth stay synchronised with each other. It's like a reset for the two realms."

"What's past the Great Forest?"

"The mountains and then nothing. Well, I put Plexiglas at the edge in case people tried to go over the mountains. I wouldn't want anyone to fall off and drop into space. Now, describe this demon."

"Ugly. Black cloak, red hat."

"Ah, Matilda." He waved his hands and suddenly the demon appeared. She looked startled as she saw the wizard and Mijestic, although with demons it was hard to read their expressions.

"Matilda that was very bad sending someone to Earth. Now, who paid you do that?"

"I cannot remember."

"Then I shall confiscate all your gold, silver and aluminium foil."

"It was Lady Jacquelyn."

"I shall have a word with her. As for you Matilda, you can no longer use that spell. Goodbye." He waved his hand and the demon disappeared.

"What did you do?"

"I sent her back to her cave where she lives. I also took away her memory of that spell."

"You can remove memories?"

"Yes. I'm sorry, but you won't be able to remember your visit to Earth, or what I just told you."

"That's not fair." Mijestic pouted. "You shouldn't just take away something from me. That's like stealing."

"What would you suggest?"

"A trade."

Salena looked at the two new pairs of shoes Mijestic brought home. "They're very nice. Vadith just gave them to you?"

"Yeah. He must like me, because he also offered to let me use his castle for my wedding!" Mijestic grinned as she held up her new shoes.

Selena frowned. "Okay, one question. You went to the market to pick some vegetables. No vegetables, but you come back with shoes. What happened? You were gone a long time."

"I don't know." Mijestic scrunched up her face as she tried to remember. I remember being followed by a demon. I must have changed my mind and somehow ended up at the shoe store."

"Well, I guess it's leftovers for dinner."

Lady Jacquelyn stood in front of Lord Montagu with her hands clasped behind her back as he sat behind his desk.

"I had a most interesting visit from Vadith. He told me you made use of the services of a demon, one that could have had disastrous consequences. Vadith had to remove part of Mijestic's memory. Apparently, she was sent to a realm outside of Elfwind, and fortunately was able to find her way back here. I say fortunately, because we do not want people from Elfwind wandering around where they don't belong."

"I'm sorry. I got jealous that she received bigger crowds than me. She's younger, prettier and I just wanted her to go away."

"That wasn't very smart of you. You shouldn't be jealous of her. Look what you have here." He spread out his arms. "Do you really want to trade places with her? I can assure you the grass isn't always greener on the other side of the valley. Sometimes that grass has a lot of weeds in it."

"You're right. I was wrong. I deserved to be punished."

"I agree. I wonder what would be a suitable punishment."

"Perhaps another courtyard session?"

"I'm thinking of a different kind of public humiliation. Assemble all the staff in the living room. You'll be tied naked while I whip you."

"Oh, yes, that sounds like very severe discipline." Lady Jacquelyn felt flush as she licked her lips.

EIGHTEEN

Lorhon stood at the door, frozen in stature and facial expression.

Mijestic held her breath as she stared at him, resisting the temptation to look down at his hands. Behind her, Lucinda, Gwendolyn and Selena waited for her to ask him to enter the home.

There was only one reason he would be at their front door. The ring. For Mijestic, this was the moment she held in anticipation for the past week. She gave a trembling smile.

"Oh, Lorhon, what a surprise. Do come in."

"Thank you." He stepped forward and gazed back at the eyes peering at him.

Mijestic escorted him to the living room, where he sat in a loveseat. He waited until the others sat down with Mijestic next to him.

"Well, this is awkward. I was planning to propose alone to Mijestic, but it seems to be a family event instead."

"She would tell us every detail anyway. This just saves us time." Gwendolyn smiled as she stared at him.

Lorhon let out a sigh and turned his attention to Mijestic.

"I didn't know what I was missing in life until I met you. You've given me a chance to see life differently, and now I can only see my life with you in it. I cannot promise you the world, but I can promise to love you, care for you and offer you all I have."

He dropped to one knee and offered the ring to her.

"Mijestic, will you be my wife?'

She didn't answer, but wrapped her arms around his neck. She sneaked a look at the ring on her finger again through wet eyes, as her mother and sisters leaned forward for a better look.

They concluded the ring was of the size and quality suitable for a princess, and Mijestic bounced around the house while holding her hand in the air.

"Isn't it beautiful?" Her question wasn't directed to anyone, and eventually Lucinda had to tell her to settle down.

"I think we all know how happy you are, but it's time to stop flaunting it around."

Mijestic grinned and gave her mother a hug.

"This was worth the wait."

Lucinda stood at the door as Mijestic and Lorhon departed. "Now who would have guessed that Mijestic would be the first of you girls to get married? I had visions of her living here for a few more decades."

Selena smiled. "Yeah, but who could have guessed that a warlock would be the one? It will be quieter here with her gone."

Gwendolyn retorted. "And more work for us."

"You're not officially mine yet." Lorhon smiled as Mijestic sat in his living room, gazing at the ring on her finger.

"That's true. We still have the marriage ceremony to do."

"Yes, and there is the collar." He held it in his hands.

Mijestic nodded. "That collar gives you great power over me."

"I do already. The collar is a symbol of it."

"True." She stood up. "I would like it if you had to catch me first before you made me wear it."

"You mean chase you around the house?"

"No, I was thinking more of you giving me a head start and I take off with my broom." She gave a shy smile. "I like the thought you need to capture me."

"Okay. But you can only wear your panties."

Mijestic considered that meant she could only fly to the Great

Forest, and not into town where flying naked would have repercussions. Lorhon's influence could only protect so much from the Justiciar.

"All right. Are you going to be undressed too?"

"No. Better hurry. You're using up your head start."

Mijestic kicked off her shoes, pulled off her top, bra and skirt. She ran to the front entrance where her broom waited, jumped on and raced off to the Great Forest. She enjoyed riding her broom almost naked, and the rush of air on her breasts caused her nipples to react. The small vibration along the broom handle penetrated between her legs, and by the time she was over the Great Forest she was already getting wet.

Mijestic accelerated her broom, looking behind her. The handle vibration increased between her legs as the broom strained to reach its top speed. Mijestic looked behind her and saw Lorhon's broom as a dark shadow in the sky, and tried changing her direction.

Shortly later she looked back. The gap between them was reduced. Mijestic tried dipping below the tree line as she began to follow the Continuous River. She bent low on the broom, and made a tight turn along a bend in the river. Mijestic looked back. To her surprise he had closed the distance quickly and she could make out his face. She made a hard turn over the river plunged down a path between the trees. The trees whipped past her and she gripped the broom handle as she made small adjustments to the curved pathway. The path opened up to a small meadow and she glanced behind her.

At first she didn't see him, thinking she had lost him, but when she looked up she he had moved above her. Lorhon was holding a coil of rope that he was waving in one hand, and at first she didn't understand what he was up to. She turned her broom again and tried to climb up, not wanting him to sit above her.

She twisted her head back, just in time to watch a loop of rope float to the end of her broom. It encircled past the straw bristles and closed tight on the shaft. Her broom suddenly jerked as the rope became taunt, and she heard the whine of her broom as it tried to get away.

She frowned as he pulled her broom back to his own while he moved it to a vertical position. Mijestic lowered her broom, knowing she wasn't getting away. She stopped on the grass and waited as he approached, carrying the collar and several leather straps.

"I guess you caught me. Are you going to take me back to the house now?"

He shook his head. "You need to be collared and tied first."

Mijestic bit her lower lip as Lorhon approached. She let her arms hang by her sides as he attached the collar around her neck, locking it with a small padlock.

She felt like she was in a trance as he folded her arms at the elbow behind her back, tying them with leather straps. He helped her to the ground and resumed tying her with the leather straps.

"Rope would cut into your skin more. The leather will make it easier to tie you tight."

Mijestic nodded. Her ankles were crossed and tied. Her broom was placed on her front and straps went from two places on her arms and around the handle. The leather also pressed on her breasts from the top and the bottom. She moaned as he wrapped a leather strap around her hips and the broom handle. She was securely tied to the broom handle, and was surprised when he held up one more length of leather. He wrapped it around her breasts, squeezing them together.

Mijestic wasn't sure why he tied her the way he did, but a few minutes later as he pulled her broom backwards with his own, she discovered his reasons. Her broom handle normally gave a small vibration as it powered its way through the air, but when it was forced to go backwards, that became a serious issue.

The throbbing between her legs caused her to alternate from moaning, gasping to groaning. The vibration was also influencing her breasts, and they tried to expand against their bonds. It was too much for Mijestic, and after a series of moans, gasps and groans, she cried out.

By the time Lorhon arrived at his home, she felt spent and lay motionless. The vibration continued to send pleasures through her body before the broom came to a rest near the front door. She rested on her back tied to the broom handle and looked up at Lorhon as he stood above her.

"I'm not done with you yet."

She became aware her broom had stopped quivering from resisting the backward travel. That disappointed her, but her broom was designed to be quiet after commands from her stopped and she didn't have the energy to order it to travel again. That became moot as Lorhon slowly pulled the broom out from her. It still left her ankles and hands tied, as well as her breasts belted together that she admitted gave them a more rounded shape. Her nipples were dark and engorged. Mijestic did the only thing she could think of. She moaned.

Lorhon ignored her sounds of pleasure as he picked her up, carrying her inside the home and to the drawing room. He stood her up near the centre of the room where a rope with a metal clip at the end hung from the ceiling.

Mijestic took in deep breaths as he passed the rope inside the leather straps that bound her breasts, and then the belt around her hips. She rocked unsteadily on her feet while he attached the rope clip to the waist of her panties, and walked to the wall. She heard a clicking sound as the rope slowly pulled upward, tugging at her panties as it dug inside her.

She moaned. The rope went higher. She groaned as she stood on her toes. The rope moved up slightly more.

"You wanted to be chased and captured. Now you're at my mercy."

"Yes." She let out a gasp as she worked to keep her feet extended.

He walked around her, holding a flogger in his hand. "You have been collared. Now you need to be disciplined. Do you disagree?"

"No, Master Lorhon." She stared at the flogger.

"Good answer."

The good answer didn't prevent him from using the flogger on her. She wondered how bad it would've been with a bad answer as the leather strips hit her up and down along her legs.

"You need to learn what will happen if you make errors. You understand I will discipline you when I feel like it?"

"Yes Master Lorhon, you have that right to decide when I need to be punished."

"That is another good answer."

Again Lorhon used the whip on her, this time working on her back, breasts and stomach.

Mijestic moaned, her skin tingling everywhere. Her feet became tired and she allowed the panties to dig into her more. *Thank goodness the fabric stretches. What else is he going to do to me?*

The answer was a hard spanking by the palm of his hand. Besides making her cheeks burn, the panties pulled with each blow. Mijestic gasped and moaned with each strike.

"Now I shall use you for my pleasure. Drop to your knees." He removed the rope from her panties.

Mijestic licked her lips as she kneeled, watching him undress. She stared at his muscles and focused on his member; the tip of the head already gleaming as it stood perpendicular from his body. He stepped toward her and she parted her lips.

He gripped her hair as he pushed inside her mouth, taking his time as he fed her his cock and slid it over her tongue. He tilted her head back, plunging his shaft into her throat, paused and pulled it out to the tip of her lips. She gulped in the air just before he repeated pushing back inside her. He repeated the slow thrusts, allowing her to take in a gasp of air. Then he began to increase his speed, holding her hair tighter, not giving her time to breathe.

Her jaw ached as she tried to accommodate his thickness. He pushed every part of his stiff erection inside, her face pressed against his skin. She felt almost smothered, waiting for him to finish. Suddenly he groaned, a guttural sound that came from deep within his being. Mijestic swallowed furiously, trying to keep up with his explosion.

He released her and as he staggered back, she collapsed on the floor. Her body ached in a hundred places. She couldn't move her limbs, her breasts pinned tightly by the leather straps and her groin a mixture of pain and needing attention. She smiled at him.

"Did I please you, Master Lorhon?"

He smiled back, "Don't act smart, or there'll be more trouble for you."

Mijestic stayed on her side as he released the leather straps and pulled off her panties.

"Do you want to rest now?"

"I do, but after I have some relief. Please, Master Lorhon?"

He scooped her up into his arms. "I'll take you to the bedroom for that."

"Hmm." Mijestic relaxed in his arms as he carried her upstairs to the bedroom. Her body felt too warm and hurt in a few sensitive places, but she was content and happy. One hand reached up and touched her collar. She sighed and closed her eyes.

In the bedroom he was gentle with her, giving every part of her body a kiss. He traced his tongue over her and his fingers manipulated her breasts. She relaxed, rolling on her stomach and back at his urging until he decided to enter her. Mijestic eagerly guided him in, pleased with the stiffness of him the second time. She came quickly, her mind replaying the events of downstairs. She lifted her arms above her head, crossing her wrists in mock bondage. As she lifted her hips against him as she moaned, crying out his name as Master Lorhon.

Mijestic woke up with Lorhon getting dressed in the room. She shifted positions, made difficult by her leash that went to the bed post.

"Good morning." She fingered the leash, knowing even though it was loosely tied to the post she wasn't allowed to remove it. "I need to use the bathroom."

"You will wear your collar during the wedding. I want you and everyone to know I'm your master." He unclipped the leash from her collar. "Understood?"

"Yes, Master Lorhon." She hurried to the bathroom, wondering how her mother would take the news she would wear a collar during the wedding. *Not likely with much joy.*

NINETEEN

The dress shop normally occupied a small room at the front of her home, but when Mijestic and her entourage arrived, Claire opened the door to the adjacent living room to accommodate everyone. Mijestic's sisters, her mother and Accalia crowded into the living room as she stood in the centre of the room. Claire used different spells to create and modify various wedding dresses, obtaining different opinions for each style.

"Claire, try making the dress backless with the see-through lace at the front." Gwendolyn gave her valued opinion on another style. The bottom of the dress was layered and flowed out at her hips, and Mijestic liked the way the material moved. It was the top portion of the dress that was causing some discussion.

The dress maker obliged, saying a few lines and the black dress Mijestic was modelling in the centre of the room changed.

Lucinda shook her head. "You're not wearing that as a wedding dress. You might as well go topless."

"Could I?" Mijestic gave a mischievous grin.

Lucinda frowned. "If you are not going to take this seriously, I will decide on a dress for you. I can assure you it will be practical and conservative."

Selena jumped in with a suggestion. "Maybe with lace at the back and a round collar at the front." She added, "With the front of opaque material."

Clair spoke a new spell and the new dress appeared on Mijestic.

Lucinda nodded. "That's better."

Mijestic looked down. "I don't like the front. You can't see the shape of my boobs at all."

Selena rolled her eyes. "You're getting married. You don't need to attract any more men. Or women."

"Can I make a suggestion?"

The women turned to Accalia who was sitting drinking tea.

"How about a V neck with the back open but tied together with string like a bodice? She would be covered but still show off her figure."

After Claire modified the dress again, there was general approval. Mijestic was happy as she examined herself in a mirror. "I like it." She fingered her collar as she twisted around in the mirror. "It's pretty and has the look of a traditional wedding dress." She smoothed down the black satin fabric.

Lucinda frowned. "I think the collar takes away from beauty of the dress. I wish you wouldn't wear it."

Mijestic sighed. "Mother, we discussed this already. Lorhon said I have to wear it and that's all there is to it. Besides, I want to show everyone that I belong to him."

"Getting married and having a ring on your finger would suffice in my opinion, which you seem so eager to ignore."

Accalia jumped to Mijestic's defence. "Actually, the collar can be seen as jewellery, kind of like a special necklace."

Lucinda stood and walked over to Mijestic, holding a hand in each one of her own. "You look beautiful. Even with that darn collar." A tear rolled down her cheek. "I'm losing my baby." She hugged Mijestic.

"But you're also gaining a son."

"Yes, who is a warlock." Lucinda sighed. "But as long as he makes you happy."

Mijestic considered a stagette a normal and reasonable activity two nights before her wedding. Having her sisters, Accalia and a few other girlfriends in the Elephant and Rook to celebrate was also reasonable. A few drinks were also reasonable. How she ended up in Richard and Accalia's backyard, naked and howling at the moon with her sisters and Accalia was bordering on the unreasonable.

Still, there she was, on her knees and howling at the moon. She wasn't as good at it as Accalia, but was better than Gwendolyn, also naked, and Selena, who was still dressed.

Accalia stood. "That was fun."

Mijestic rolled over on her back. "It was, but I'm getting a sore throat. Now what do we do?" She slurred her words.

Gwendolyn agreed. "I think it's time we dragged Mijestic home."

Accalia shook her head. "Good luck in getting her to fly on a broom now. She can spend the night here." She took Mijestic's hand. "As a matter of fact, none of you are in a condition to fly home. Come on, let's go inside."

"Is there more beer?" Mijestic asked as she staggered toward the house.

Selena and Gwendolyn helped Accalia guide Mijestic into the house, creating noise as they bumped into anything that wasn't part of the floor.

Accalia pointed at the couch. "You can sleep on that, or there's an extra bedroom down the hall. No bed in there, but you can take some blankets and make yourself comfortable. Just ignore the stuff in there."

Gwendolyn dropped on the couch. "That's okay. I can sleep here."

Selena curled up in the armchair. "I'll sleep in here with Gwen. What about Mijestic?"

"I'll take care of her." Accalia pulled Mijestic by the hand to the bedroom.

"Where's the beer? I need another drink."

"You need sleep." Accalia pushed Mijestic into the bed. "Try not to wake Richard."

"I like Richard." Mijestic slid against him, dropping her head on his chest.

Richard grumbled about being disturbed, and then grunted as Mijestic wrapped her fingers around his now stiffening penis.

"I'm sorry, I can't give you a blow job without Lorhon's permission." She took in a deep breath. "I'm tired."

Richard listened to the regular breathing of Mijestic, and saw Accalia's arm draped over her. His erection was being held in Mijestic's grasp as she slept. "Lords of Middle Earth. How am I supposed to go to sleep now?"

Despite not having a good sleep, punctuated by vivid dreams, Richard was the first one up. His erection refused to go down and he gave up trying to pull on his jeans. He quietly went to the bathroom and then to the kitchen to make strong tea.

He tossed wood into the stove, lit it, filled the kettle and leaned back against the counter to wait for the water to boil. Richard wasn't quiet as he prepared the stove, not worried he might disturb Accalia and Mijestic. His mind was on the activity he would require Accalia to perform when Selena and Gwendolyn entered the kitchen.

They stared at him. They gasped, covering their mouths but not their eyes. They continued to stare.

Richard wasn't sure what he could do to cover himself, but did the next best thing. He greeted them.

"Good morning. I'm Richard, but I believe we've met before. Would you care for some tea when it's ready?"

Gwendolyn continued to stare. "Tea?"

Selena gave her sister a poke. "Gwen, stop acting like an idiot. Sorry, Richard. We were expecting to see Accalia and were going ask how Mijestic was doing. We'll go back to the living room and give you some privacy." She tried to turned Gwendolyn around, who kept twisting her back to look at him. Selena grabbed her hand and pulled her back to the living room.

As soon as they left, Richard headed back to the bedroom to get dressed. "Amazing, the one time I go to the kitchen naked, two women appear." He looked at Accalia and Mijestic. "And unlike those two, dressed."

He gave Accalia a smack on her rear as she lay on her side. "Come on, wake up. You have guests here that I do not need to entertain anymore."

Richard made breakfast. Unlike Selena and Gwendolyn, he wasn't embarrassed on seeing them at the table. Gwendolyn kept looking at him, blushing every time he saw her staring. Accalia was being extra polite to everyone, and helped serve the food, knowing Richard would hold her responsible for the morning surprise.

Mijestic was slumped in her chair, eating little and drinking lots of tea.

Accalia put her hand on her shoulder. "Is there anything I can get you? You look tired."

"I've a craving for a latte."

"What's a latte?"

"I don't know, but I want one."

Mijestic's broom lagged behind the others. The spell she used cured most of the hangover, but there were lingering effects.

Lucinda didn't say much to her daughters, other than asking if they had a good time. She smiled when she saw Mijestic stumble into the living room and collapsed onto the couch.

"You just take easy now. You have a big day tomorrow. Would you like me to get you anything? Tea? Something to eat?"

Selena whispered to Gwendolyn. "How to get on mother's good side. Just get married."

TWENTY

The mayor's castle was large, expensively decorated and filled with wedding guests. Mijestic barely noticed, pacing around in a bedroom after receiving help from her sisters and Accalia to get dressed.

Selena pushed her down in an armchair. "Settle down. Do you want to marry him or not?"

"I do."

"Then stop pacing around like a cat in heat. You made a decision, so stop worrying about it."

Mijestic nodded. "It's just that it's the biggest day of my life."

"Then enjoy it."

"You're right. I'm just nervous." Mijestic smiled. "Thanks." She rubbed Selena's arm.

Lucinda entered the bedroom. "It's time. If you want to back out, I'll go make a statement for you."

"I'm ready to get married. No second guesses."

Mijestic went downstairs with her mother leading the way. The ballroom was filled with people who all turned their attention to the bride as she entered the room. A string quartet played an interesting edition of 'Here Comes the Bride'. Mijestic made a slow walk to the room's centre, where Lorhon and the priest waited. Lucinda, Mijestic's sisters and Accalia joined the others as they made a circle around the couple.

The priest made an introduction, greeted the assembly and explained the importance of marriage.

Mijestic thought he must enjoy the sound of his own voice, as he described not only marriage, but a story of how his grandparents met and their marriage. He told of the four corners of the world and their significance. He spoke about sun, the moon and all the planets. He spoke about how life comes from the soil. He spoke longer than some marriages lasted.

Finally, Mijestic joined hands with Lorhon and Accalia used a thin rope to tie their wrists together.

"Now they are joined together, to face their new life as one." He waited as Gwendolyn and Selena each grabbed an end of a broom, holding it knee high above the floor. "Now Mijestic and Lorhon will now jump over the broom, leaving their separate lives behind them and entering a new one as husband and wife."

Mijestic jumped over the broom. Normally such a jump wouldn't be difficult, but a long wedding dress presented some problems. She used one hand to gather up as much fabric as possible and made the leap. Lorhon immediately took her in his arms and gave her a long kiss.

Congratulations, handshakes, hugs and kisses were extended to the happy couple. Mijestic was given a drink and she chatted with the well-wishers, including the mayor, who seemed amused at her grateful thanks for the offer of the use of the castle for the wedding.

"That is all right, my dear. Vadith explained to me it was part of an agreement he made with you. It seems you're a very good at getting what you want."

Mijestic smiled and went to rescue Lorhon, who was surrounded by admiring females.

"I see you're keeping yourself entertained."

Lorhon nodded. "I'm glad you found me. Your mother wants to see us. It seems she has something for us."

Mijestic slipped her hand inside his arm and walked with him to where her mother was chatting with a few witches and warlocks. Despite some apprehension by Lucinda, it seemed the two guilds didn't want to fight. Rather it was quite the opposite with friendly introductions being exchanged.

Lucinda excused herself and led Mijestic and Lorhon to a spare bedroom, one of two dozen bedrooms the castle contained. As they walked, Mijestic's sisters and Accalia hurried to catch up. A few steps behind them Richard followed.

Mijestic wondered what was going on. *Whatever it is, my sisters and Accalia are aware what it is.*

Inside the bedroom Lucinda smiled and presented a small wood box to Mijestic.

"This is a special gift for you and Lorhon."

Mijestic took the box and opened the lid.

"We hand it down to the first married daughter. I'm sure you will find it very useful."

Mijestic reached inside the box and produced the famous hairbrush.

Lorhon smiled. "Yes, there'll most certainly be a use for it."

Gwendolyn spoke up, "There's no time like the present."

Selena agreed. "We didn't come in here just to watch you open the box."

Accalia took her hand and pulled her to where Lorhon stood by the edge of the bed. She took the hairbrush and passed it to Lorhon. "You have a job to do."

Mijestic saw Lorhon had sat on the bed and eased over his lap. She felt him pull up the mounds of material of her dress until he laid bare her backside. His hand touched the inside of her thigh and she spread her legs. Mijestic followed Lorhon's previous order and was without panties, which meant she was giving a view to the others she would have preferred not to. Still, everyone in the room had seen her naked before and she was getting used to being spanked in front of others.

The hairbrush hit her cheeks in powerful strokes, and although Lorhon was holding back, she cried out. He stopped after only ten strokes, to the applause of the others in the room.

Lucinda spoke. "Well done, son-in-law. She is now officially your responsibility to keep in line. My responsibility now is for her two sisters. For that, I need to get a new hairbrush."

Mijestic, blushing as she straightened out her dress, gazed at Lorhon.

"Thank you. I now feel truly married to you."

He stood and kissed her. "And you're going to feel married to me for a long time."

The end.

Don't miss out on your next favorite book!

Join the Melange Books mailing list at
www.melange-books.com/mail.html

AUTHOR'S NOTE

In Chapter Two we are introduced to Constable Moe Thursday, badge number 417. This is an acknowledgement to the old Dragnet series, Joe Friday, badge number 714.

In Chapter Three there was reference to the beautiful language the ancients used. The language is Ukrainian.

Є пляма я потребую позбутися
  Чи викликаний відрізком часу або не.
  Зробіть це imperfection поїдьте Таким чином
  я буду красивий ще раз весь день.

There is a spot I need to get rid of
  Whether caused by a time segment or not.
  Make this imperfection go way
  I'll be beautiful once more all day.

Names: If you're curious where the names I used came from, I've listed some below.

Enyo, Mijestic's torturer: Goddess, in Greek mythology, of war and destruction.

Accalia: The name of the human foster mother of Romulus and Remus, the twins who founded Rome. Legend has it that after their abandonment as infants, they were initially suckled by a she-wolf. Accalia was her replacement. It is a bit of a stretch but I decided it was a good name for a werewolf.

Varulv: The alpha werewolf who married Accalia and Richard. Varulv means werewolf in Norwegian.

Vadith: According to name definition: "Born to be an executive. If they have true passion for something, they can give everything for it." Thus, I made him the Grand Wizzard.

Lilith: I took her name from the bible. Depending on which version you read, she is often written as sinful. "Lilith represents chaos, seduction and ungodliness."

Theron. Mijestic's lover: In Greek, Theron means hunter and untamed- a good name for a warlock.

Lucinda, Mijestic's mother: Mythological Roman goddess of childbirth and giver of first light to new borns. Also refers to Mary as Lady of the Light.

Justiciar: A high judicial officer in medieval England.

Walpurgis Night: From Collins Dictionary. "When witches supposedly gathered on Brocken mountain for a demonic orgy."

THANK YOU FOR READING

Did you enjoy this book?

We invite you to leave a review at the website of your choice, such as Goodreads, Amazon, Barnes & Noble, etc.

DID YOU KNOW THAT LEAVING A REVIEW...

- Helps other readers find books they may enjoy.
- Gives you a chance to let your voice be heard.
- Gives authors recognition for their hard work.
- Doesn't have to be long. A sentence or two about why you liked the book will do.

ABOUT THE AUTHOR

Nick Howard lives near Grande Prairie, Alberta where winter is never far away. There he pursues a dream of writing and taming weeds on an acreage. So far the weeds are winning but perhaps the writing will allow him to feel a small measure of victory.

He shares the green jungle with his wife, and a dog that thinks itself as human. Rumors that the dog assists him in writing are greatly exaggerated as the dog is horrible at grammar.

www.nshoward.com
nshwrd@yahoo.ca

ALSO BY N. S. HOWARD

www.ingramcontent.com/pod-product-compliance
Lightning Source LLC
Chambersburg PA
CBHW030337180626
46810CB00003B/1391